To Pete, at the start of
something new and wonderful —
חזוכה שלא!
& happy reading,
Ariel.

the

bus driver

who wanted

to be god

and
other
stories

the
bus
driver
who
wanted
to be
god

and
other
stories

ETGAR
KERET

THOMAS DUNNE BOOKS
st. martin's press
new york

THOMAS DUNNE BOOKS.
An imprint of St. Martin's Press.

All stories translated by Miriam Shlesinger except for "Breaking the Pig," "The Flying Santinis," "Korbi's Girl," "Missing Kissinger," translated by Dalya Bilu; "Shoes," translated by Margaret Weinberger Rotman; "Siren," translated by Anthony Berris; "Jetlag," translated by Dan Ofri.

Book design by Tim Hall

ISBN 0-312-26188-8

First Edition: October 2001

10 9 8 7 6 5 4 3 2 1

To Eyal and Shlomo

contents

the

bus driver

who wanted

to be god

and
other
stories

opening the door for someone who came late was just under thirty seconds, and if not opening the door meant that this person would wind up losing fifteen minutes of his life, it would still be more fair to society to not open the door, because the thirty seconds would be lost by every single passenger on the bus. And if there were, say, sixty people on the bus who hadn't done anything wrong and had all arrived at the bus stop on time, then together they'd be losing half a hour, which is double fifteen minutes. This was the only reason why he'd never open the door. He knew that the passengers hadn't the slightest idea what his reason was, and that the people running after the bus and signaling him to stop had no idea either. He also knew that most of them thought he was just an SOB, and that personally it would have been much much easier for him to let them on and receive their smiles and thanks. Except that when it came to choosing between smiles and thanks on the one hand, and the good of society on the other, this driver knew what it had to be.

The person who should have suffered the most from the driver's ideology was named Eddie, but unlike the other people in this story, he wouldn't even try to run for the bus; that's how lazy and wasted he was. Now, Eddie was assistant cook at a restaurant called the Steakaway, which was the best pun that the stupid owner of the place could come up with. The food there was nothing to write home about, but Eddie himself was a really nice guy—so nice that sometimes when something he made didn't come out too great, he'd serve it to the table himself and apologize. It was during one of these apologies that he met Happiness, or at least a shot at Happiness, in the form of a girl who was so sweet that she tried to finish the entire portion of roast beef that he brought her, just so he wouldn't feel bad. And this girl didn't want to tell him her name or give him her phone number, but she was sweet enough to agree to meet him the next day at five at a spot they decided on together—at the Dolphinarium, to be exact.

Now Eddie had this condition—one that had already caused him to miss out on all sorts of things in life. It wasn't one of those conditions where your adenoids get all swollen or anything like that, but still, it had already caused him a lot of damage. This sickness always made him oversleep by ten minutes, and no alarm clock did any good. That was why he was invariably late for work at the Steakaway—that and our bus driver, the one who always chose the good of society over positive reinforcements on the individual level. Except that this time, since Happiness was at stake, Eddie decided to beat the condition, and instead of taking an afternoon nap he stayed awake and watched television. Just to be on the safe

side, he even lined up not one but three alarm clocks
and ordered a wake-up call to boot. But this sickness
was incurable, and Eddie fell asleep like a baby,
watching the kiddie channel. He woke up in a sweat
to the screeching of a trillion million alarm clocks—
ten minutes too late—rushed out of the house without stopping to change, and ran toward the bus stop.
He barely remembered how to run anymore, and his
feet fumbled a bit every time they left the sidewalk.
The last time he ran was before he discovered that
he could cut gym class, which was about in the sixth
grade, except that unlike in those gym classes, this
time he ran like crazy, because now he had something to lose, and all the pains in his chest and his
Lucky Strike wheezing weren't going to get in the
way of his pursuit of Happiness. Nothing was going
to get in his way except our bus driver, who had
just closed the door and was beginning to pull away.
The driver saw Eddie in the rearview mirror, but as
we've already explained, he had an ideology—a well-
reasoned ideology that, more than anything, relied
on a love of justice and on simple arithmetic. Except
that Eddie didn't care about the driver's arithmetic.
For the first time in his life, he really wanted to get
somewhere on time. And that's why he went right on
chasing the bus, even though he didn't have a
chance.

Suddenly, Eddie's luck turned, but only halfway:

one hundred yards past the bus stop there was a traffic light. And just a second before the bus reached it, the traffic light turned red. Eddie managed to catch up with the bus and drag himself all the way to the driver's door. He didn't even bang on the glass, he was so weak. He just looked at the driver with moist eyes and fell to his knees, panting and wheezing. And this reminded the driver of something—something from out of the past, from a time even before he wanted to become a bus driver, when he still wanted to become God. It was kind of a sad memory, because the driver didn't become God in the end, but it was a happy one too, because he became a bus driver, which was his second choice. And suddenly the driver remembered how he'd once promised himself that if he became God in the end, He'd be merciful and kind and would listen to all His creatures. So when he saw Eddie from way up in his driver's seat, kneeling on the asphalt, he simply couldn't go through with it, and in spite of all his ideology and his simple arithmetic he opened the door, and Eddie got on—and didn't even say thank-you, he was so out of breath.

The best thing would be to stop reading here, because even though Eddie did get to the Dolphinarium on time, Happiness couldn't come, because Happiness already had a boyfriend. It's just that she was so sweet that she couldn't bring herself to tell

goodman

About six months ago, in this armpit town outside Austin, Texas, Mickey Goodman of Tel Aviv killed a seventy-year-old minister and his wife. Goodman shot them in their sleep at point-blank range. To this day nobody knows how he got into the apartment, but he must have had a key. The whole story sounds too far out. I mean how does a guy with no record, an Israeli paratrooper, just get up one morning and put a slug into the heads of two people he's never even met, in some armpit town in Texas— and someone called Goodman no less. The night they announced it on the news I didn't even know, because I was with Alma at the movies. Later, in bed, we were really getting into it when suddenly she started crying. I stopped right away, cause I thought I was hurting her, but she said I should go on and that her crying was a good sign, actually.

The prosecution said Goodman had been paid thirty thousand for the murder and that the whole thing had to do with some local feud over an inheritance. Fifty years ago the fact that the minister and his wife were black would only have helped him, but nowadays it's the other way around. The fact that the old man was a minister also worked against him. His attorney announced that after the trial, if Goodman was found guilty, he'd ask to serve out his sentence back home in Israel, because with all the blacks in U.S. prisons, his life wouldn't be worth a used tea bag. The prosecution, on the other hand, claimed that Goodman would be dead much sooner, anyway. Texas is one of the few states where they still have capital punishment.

I haven't had any contact with Goodman for ten years now, but back in high school he used to be my best friend. I'd spend all my time with him and with Dafne, his girlfriend back in junior high. Once we got into the army, we lost touch. I'm no good at keeping tabs on people. Alma's great at it, though. Her best friends are people she's known since kindergarten. I kind of envy her for that.

The trial lasted three months. Loads of time considering that everyone was convinced Goodman did

thought that was a pretty awful thing to do, and that Goodman didn't exactly come across as a nice guy in that story, either. The worst thing Alma ever did was while she was in the army. Her commander, who was fat and repulsive, kept trying to ball her, and she hated him, especially because he was married and his wife was pregnant at the time. "Get the picture?" She took a drag on her cigarette. "His wife's carrying his baby around inside her, and all he wants the whole time is to fuck other women." Her commander was totally hung up on her, so she made the most of it and told him she'd agree to do it with him, but only if he paid a bundle, a thousand shekels, which looked like a lot to her back then. "I didn't care about the money," she cringed as she recalled. "I just wanted to humiliate him. To make him feel like no woman would have him unless he paid. If there's one thing I hate, it's men who cheat." Her commander arrived with a thousand shekels in an envelope, except he was so excited that he couldn't get it up. But Alma wouldn't give him his money back, which made the humiliation twice as bad. She told me his money disgusted her so much that she buried it in some savings plan, and to this very day she won't go near it.

The ending of the trial came as a surprise, for me at least, and Goodman got the death sentence. The Japanese announcer on CNN said the prisoner had cried quietly when he heard the verdict. My mother said he had it coming, and my father said the same thing he always says: "You never know what goes on in people's heads." The second I heard about the sentence, I knew I had to fly over there and visit him before they killed him. We used to be best friends once, after all. It was kind of strange, but everyone except my mother understood. My older brother, Ari, asked me to smuggle in a laptop on my way back from America and said that if worse came to worse I could just leave it in customs and go.

In Texas I went straight from the airport to Mickey's prison. I'd set it up before I left. They gave me half an hour. When I went in to meet him, he was sitting on a chair. His hands and legs were tied up. The guards said they had to tie him up because he kept going wild, but he seemed perfectly calm to me. I think that they were just saying it, that they just got their kicks from coming down on him. I sat facing him. Everything seemed so ordinary. The first thing he said to me was, "Sorry." He said he felt bad about what happened at Dafne's funeral. "I was just plain mean to you," he said. "Shouldn't have done that." I told him it was ancient history. "It must have been bugging me for a long time, and suddenly, with her death and all, it just came out. It wasn't because you were sleeping with her behind my back, I swear to you. It's just because you broke her heart." I told him to cut the crap, but I couldn't make my voice not tremble. "Forget it," he said. "She told me, and I forgave you long ago. The whole business at the funeral—take it from me, I was acting like a jerk." I asked him about the murder, but he didn't want to talk about it, so we talked about other things. After twenty minutes, the guard said the half hour was up.

They used to execute people by electrocution, and when they'd throw the switch, the lights in the whole area would flicker for a few seconds and everyone would stop what they were doing, just like when there's a special news flash. I thought about it, how I'd sit in my hotel room and the lights would go dim, but it didn't happen. Nowadays they use a lethal injection, so nobody can even tell when it's happening. They said it would be on the hour. I looked at the second hand on my watch, and when it reached twelve I told myself: "He must be dead now." The truth is that I was the one who wrote the graffiti on Sarah's wall. Mickey had just watched. I think he was even kind of against it. And now he was probably not alive anymore.

On the return flight, the seat next to me was taken by this fat guy. His seat was a little broken but the attendants couldn't move him to a different one because the flight was full. His name was Pelleg, and he told me he'd just gotten out of the army with the rank of lieutenant colonel, and he was returning from a special course where they train people for senior executive positions in hi-tech.

I looked at him leaning back, with his eyes closed, struggling to find a comfortable position in his broken seat, when suddenly it came to me that maybe this guy could have been Alma's commander in the army. Her commander was fat, too. I could picture him waiting for her in some stinking hotel room, his sweaty hands counting up the thousand shekels. Thinking about the lay that was to happen, about his wife, about the baby. Trying to give himself some excuse, why it's really OK after all.

I looked at him squirming in his seat beside me. His eyes were shut the whole time, but he wasn't asleep. Then he gave a kind of groan, for no reason. Maybe he was remembering it, too. I dunno, suddenly I felt sorry for the guy.

hole in the wall

On Bernadotte Avenue, right next to the Central Bus Station, there's a hole in the wall. There used to be an ATM there once, but it broke or something, or else nobody ever used it, so the people from the bank came in a pickup and took it and never brought it back.

Somebody once told Udi that if you scream a wish into this hole it comes true, but Udi didn't really buy that. The truth is that once, on his way home from the movies, he screamed into the hole in the wall that he wanted Ruth Rimalt to fall in love with him, and nothing happened. And once, when he was feeling really lonely, he screamed into the hole in the wall that he wanted to have an angel for a friend, and an angel really did show up right after that, but he was never much of a friend, and he'd always disappear just when Udi really needed him. This angel was skinny and all stooped and he wore a trench coat the whole time to hide his wings. People in the street were sure he was a hunchback. Sometimes, when there were just the two of them, he'd take the coat off. Once he even let Udi touch the feathers on his wings. But when there was anyone else in the room, he always kept it on. Klein's kids asked him once what he had under his coat, and he said it was a backpack full of books that didn't belong to him and that he didn't want them to get wet. Actually, he lied all the time. He told Udi such stories you could die: about places in heaven, about people who when they go to bed at night leave the keys in the ignition, about cats who aren't afraid of anything and don't even know the meaning of "scat." The stories he made up were something else, and to top it all, he'd cross-his-heart-and-hope-to-die.

Udi was nuts about him and always tried hard to believe him. Even lent him some money a couple of times when he was hard up. As for the angel, he didn't do a thing to help Udi. He just talked and talked and talked, rambling off his harebrained stories. In the six years he knew him, Udi never saw him so much as rinse a glass.

When Udi was in basic training and really needed

someone to talk to, the angel suddenly disappeared on him for two solid months. Then he came back with an unshaven, don't-ask-what-happened face. So Udi didn't ask, and on Saturday they sat around on the roof in their underpants just taking in the sun and feeling low. Udi looked at the other rooftops with the cable hookups and the solar heaters and the sky. It occurred to him suddenly that in all their years together he'd never once seen the angel fly.

"How about flying around a little," he said to the angel. "It would make you feel better."

And the angel said: "Forget it. What if someone sees me?"

"Be a sport," Udi nagged. "Just a little. For my sake." But the angel just made this disgusting noise from the inside of his mouth and shot a gob of spit and white phlegm at the tar-covered roof.

"Never mind," Udi sulked. "I bet you don't know how to fly, anyway."

"Sure I do," the angel shot back. "I just don't want people to see me, that's all."

On the roof across the way they saw some kids throwing a water bomb. "You know," Udi smiled. "Once, when I was little, before I met you, I used to come up here a lot and throw water bombs on people in the street below. I'd aim them into the space between that awning and the other one," he explained, bending over the railing and pointing down at the narrow gap between the awning over the grocery store and the one over the shoe store. "People would look up, and all they'd see was the awning. They wouldn't know where it was coming from."

The angel got up too and looked down into the street. He opened his mouth to say something. Suddenly, Udi gave him a little shove from behind, and the angel lost his balance. Udi was just fooling around. He didn't really mean to hurt the angel, just to make him fly a little, for laughs. But the angel dropped the whole five floors, like a sack of potatoes. Stunned, Udi watched him lying there on the sidewalk below. His whole body was completely still, except the wings, which were still fluttering a little, like when someone dies. That's when he finally understood that of all the things the angel had told him, nothing was true. That he wasn't even an angel, just a liar with wings.

exact profile. Fat/thin, with/without a moustache—
a very mixed crowd. If they have anything in com-
mon at all, it's the way they act. They're all kind of
quiet and polite, always giving you the exact change
and everything. They never try to haggle over prices,
and they always know just what they want—no hem-
ming and hawing. They come in, ask how much, gift
wrap/no gift wrap, and that's that. They're all kind
of very short-term guests, spending the day and then
going back to Hell. And you never see the same one
twice, cause they only come out every one hundred
years. That's just how it is. Those are the rules. Like
in the army when you only get one weekend off out
of three, or on guard duty, when you're only allowed
to sit down for five minutes every hour on the hour.
It's the same with the people in Hell: one day off
every hundred years. If there ever was an explana-
tion, nobody remembers it anymore. By now it's
more a matter of maintaining the status quo.

Anna had worked in her grandfather's grocery
store for as long as she could remember. Apart from
the villagers, there weren't that many customers, but
once every few hours someone would come in smelling of sulfur and ask for a pack of cigarettes, or choc-
olate, or whatever. Some of them asked for things
that they'd probably never actually seen and had only
heard about from some other sinner. So every once
in a while she'd see them struggle to open a can of

Coke or try to eat cheese with the plastic wrapper still on it. Things like that. Sometimes she'd try to chat them up, to make friends, but they never knew Uzbek or whatever you call the language she spoke. And in the end, it would always wind up that she'd just point to herself and say "Anna" and they'd point to themselves and mumble "Maximus" or "Su-Ying" or "Steve" or "Avi," and then they'd pay and take off. So she'd see them again later that evening, cruising the neighborhood or hanging out on some street corner, staring out into the evening sky, and the next day she wouldn't see them anymore. Her grandfather, who suffered from a condition that wouldn't let him sleep more than an hour a night, would tell her how he'd see them at dawn going back down through the opening that was right next to their front porch. It was from this same porch that he also saw her father, who was a pretty nasty piece of work, going down through the opening like the others, stone drunk, and singing some really off-color song. Ninety-odd years later he too was supposed to come back for a day.

Funny, but you could say these people were the most interesting thing in Anna's life. Their faces, the ridiculous clothes, the attempts to guess what terrible thing they were supposed to have done to deserve Hell. 'Cause the truth is that it really was the only thing going on. Sometimes, when she got bored in the shop, she'd try to picture the next sinner who'd walk through the door. She'd always try to imagine them very good-looking or funny. And once every few weeks there really might be some gorgeous hunk or else some guy who'd insist on eating the contents of a can without opening it first, and then she and her grandfather would talk about it for days.

Once, this guy walked in who was so gorgeous that she knew she simply had to be with him. He bought some white wine, some soda water, and all sorts of hot spices, and instead of adding up his bill, she just took him by the hand and pulled him toward the house. And the guy, without understanding a word she was saying, followed her and tried his very best, but when they both realized that he just couldn't, Anna hugged him and gave him her biggest smile, to make sure he understood it didn't really matter. But that didn't help, and he cried right through the night. From the moment he left, she prayed every night for him to come back and for everything to be alright. She was praying more for him than for herself, and when she told her grandfather about it, he smiled and said she had a good heart.

Two months later he was back. He came into the shop and bought a pastrami sandwich, and when she smiled at him he smiled back. Her grandfather said it couldn't be him, because everyone knows they only come out once every hundred years, and that it must be his twin or something, and she wasn't really completely sure, either. In any case, when they got into bed, things actually went fine. He seemed content, and so did she. And suddenly she understood that maybe it wasn't only him that she was praying for after all. Later, he went into the kitchen and found the bag he'd left behind the last time, with the soda water and the spices and the wine, and he took it and mixed a drink for Anna and himself that was fizzy and hot and cold, and wine, too. A kind of spritzer from Hell.

When the night was over and he was getting dressed to go, she asked him not to, and he shrugged like someone who had no choice. And after he left, she prayed he'd come a third time, if it was really him, and if not, that someone would come who looked enough like him that she'd be able to make the same mistake. And a few weeks later, when she started throwing up, she prayed it would be a baby, but it turned out just to be a virus. It was just about then that people in the village began talking about plans to close up the opening from the inside. This had Anna very worried, but her grandfather said it was just a rumor being spread by people who had nothing better to do. "You've got nothing to worry about," he said and smiled at her. "That opening has been there for so long that neither devil nor angel would ever have the nerve to close it." And she believed him, except one particular night, she remembers, when she suddenly felt, for no special reason, and it wasn't even in her sleep, that the opening wasn't there anymore. She ran out in her nightgown and was happy to see that it still was. And then, she remembers, there was a moment when she had this urge to go down there. She felt as though she was being sucked in, because of how she felt about her special visitor, or maybe because she really wanted to see her father, who was a nasty piece of work, or maybe more than anything, it was because she didn't want to go on being alone in this boring village. She put her ear to the cold air coming out of the opening. In the distance she could make out something that sounded like people screaming, or water running—it was impossible to tell just what it was. It was coming from really far away. Eventually she went back to bed, and a few days later the opening really did disappear. Hell continued to exist down below, but nobody came out anymore.

Ever since the opening disappeared, it became harder to make ends meet, and also much more tired and serene. Her grandfather died, she married the fishmonger's son, and the two shops merged. They had several children, and she loved to tell them stories, especially ones about the people who used to walk into the shop, smelling of sulfur. Those stories would scare them, and they'd start to cry. But still, even though she couldn't understand why, she went right on telling them.

who stays with a woman who's no woman is no man himself," he told my older brother and me a second before he got onto the plane to Alaska. "When you grow up, you'll understand."

The room where they had my mom's uterus on display was all dark. The only light came from the uterus itself, which shone with a kind of gentle glow, like the inside of a plane on a night flight. In pictures it didn't look like anything much, because of the flash, but when I saw it up close I could understand perfectly well why it had the doctor in tears. "You came out of there," my uncle said and pointed. "You were like princes living in there, believe me. What a mother you had, what a mother."

Eventually my mother died. Eventually all mothers die. And my dad became a famous arctic explorer and whaler. The girls I dated always used to take it the wrong way when I'd peek at their uterus. They thought it was some kind of gynecological hangup, which is a definite turnoff. But one of them, with a good sturdy build, agreed to marry me. I used to spank our kids a lot, right from infancy, because their crying got on my nerves. And the truth is they learned their lessons fast and stopped crying for good by the time they were nine months, if not earlier. In the beginning I'd take them to the museum on their birthdays to show them their grandmother's uterus, but they didn't really get into it, and my wife would be pissed off, so little by little I started taking them to Walt Disney movies instead.

One day my car was towed, and the police lot was in the same neighborhood, so I dropped in at the museum while I was there. The uterus wasn't in its usual place. They'd moved it to a room on the side, full of old pictures, and when I took a closer look I saw it was all covered with tiny green dots. I asked the guard why nobody was keeping it clean, but he just shrugged. I begged the guy in charge of the exhibition to let me clean it off myself if they were short-staffed, but the guy in charge was very nasty. He said I wasn't allowed to touch the exhibits because I wasn't a member of the staff. My wife said the museum was one hundred percent right, and that as far as she was concerned, displaying a uterus in a public institution is sick, especially when the place is full of children, but I couldn't think of anything else. Deep in my heart I knew that if I didn't break into the museum, steal it out of there and take care of it, I'd stop being what I am. Just like my dad that night, on the steps of the plane, I knew exactly what I had to do.

Two days later, I took a van from work and arrived at the museum just before it closed. The rooms were empty, but even if I had met someone, it wouldn't have worried me. I was armed this time, and besides, I had a really good plan. My only problem was that the uterus itself had disappeared. The guy in charge of the exhibition was kind of surprised to see me, but when I shoved the butt of my new Jericho deep in his throat he was very quick to cough up the information. The uterus had been sold the day before to a Jewish philanthropist, who had stipulated that it should be sent to one of the community centers in Alaska. On the way there, it had been hijacked by a few people from the local chapter of the Ecological Front. The Front issued a press release announcing that a uterus doesn't belong in captivity, which was why they'd decided to set it free in natural surroundings. According to Reuters, this Ecological Front was radical and dangerous. Its whole operation was run from a pirate ship commanded by a retired whaler. I thanked the guy in charge and put away my gun. The whole way home, all the lights were red. I just kept swerving from lane to lane without bothering to look in the mirror, struggling to get rid of the lump that stuck in my throat. I tried to imagine my mother's uterus in the middle of a green, dew-covered field, floating in an ocean full of dolphins and tuna.

Every morning I have to drink a cup of cocoa, even though I hate it. Cocoa with skin is a shekel, without skin it's half a shekel, and if I throw up right away I don't get anything. I put the coins into the pig's back, and when you shake it, it rattles. When the pig is full and it doesn't rattle when you shake it I'll get Bart Simpson on a skateboard. That's what Dad says; that way it's educational. Actually the pig's cute, his nose is cold when you touch it, and he smiles when you push the shekel into his back and when you push in half a shekel too, but the nicest thing is that he smiles even when you don't. I gave him a name; I called him Margolis, after a man who used to live in our mailbox—and my Dad couldn't peel off his label. Margolis isn't like my other toys, he's much calmer, without lights and springs and batteries that leak. Only you have to watch that he doesn't jump off the table. "Margolis, be careful! You're made of porcelain," I remind him when I catch him bending down a bit to look at the floor, and he smiles at me and waits patiently for me to take him down myself. I love it when he smiles; it's only because of him that I drink the cocoa with the skin every morning, so that I can push the shekel into his back and watch how his smile doesn't change at all. "I love you, Margolis," I tell him afterward. "Honest, I love you more than Mom and Dad. And I'll always love you, no matter what, even if you break into candy stores. But don't even think of jumping off the table!"

Yesterday Dad came and picked Margolis up off the table, began to shake him wildly and to turn him upside down. "Be careful, Dad," I said to him, "you're giving Margolis a tummy ache." But Dad didn't stop. "It's not making a noise anymore. You know what that means, don't you? Tomorrow you'll get a Bart Simpson on a skateboard." "That's great, Dad," I said, "a Bart Simpson on a skateboard, great. Just stop shaking Margolis, it's making him dizzy." Dad put Margolis back on the table and went to call Mom. He came back a minute later, pulling her with one hand and holding a hammer in the other. "See, I was right," he said to Mom, "now he knows that things have value. Right, Yoavi?" "Sure I do," I said. "Sure, but what's the hammer for?" "It's for you," said Dad and put the hammer in my hand. "Just be careful." "Sure I'll be careful," I said, and I was, but after a few minutes Dad got fed up and said, "Go on, then, break the pig." "What?" I asked. "Break Margolis?" "Yes, yes, Margolis," said Dad. "Go on, break it. You've earned the Bart Simpson, you've worked hard enough for it." Margolis smiled at me with the sad smile of a porcelain pig who knows his end is near.

To hell with the Bart Simpson. Me hit a friend on the head with a hammer? "I don't want the Bart Simpson." I gave Dad the hammer back. "Margolis is enough for me." "You don't understand," said Dad. "It's all right, it's educational, come on, I'll break it for you." Dad was lifting the hammer. Looking at Mom's crushed eyes and Margolis's tired smile, I knew it was up to me. If I didn't do something, he was dead. "Dad." I grabbed him by the leg. "What is it, Yoavi?" said Dad, his hammer-hand poised in midair. "May I have another shekel, please," I begged. "One more shekel to push inside him, tomorrow, after the cocoa. And then we'll break him, tomorrow, I promise." "Another shekel?" Dad smiled and put the hammer down. "You see? The boy has learned self-restraint." "Yes, self-restraint," I said. "Tomorrow." There were tears in my throat already.

When they left the room I hugged Margolis very tight and let the tears out. He didn't say anything, only trembled quietly in my hands. "Don't worry," I whispered in his ear, "I'll save you."

That night I waited for Dad to finish watching TV in the living room and go to bed. Then I got up very quietly and sneaked out through the porch with Margolis. We walked in the dark for a long time, until we reached a thorny field. "Pigs are crazy about fields," I told Margolis as I put him down on the ground, "especially fields with thorns. You'll like it here." I waited for an answer, but Margolis didn't say any-thing, and when I touched him on the nose to say good-bye he just gave me a sad look. He knew he'd never see me again.

cocked and locked

He's standing there in the middle of the alleyway, about twenty meters away from me, his kaffiyeh over his face, trying to provoke me to come closer: "Zbecial Force cocksucker," he shouts at me in a heavy Arabic accent.

"What's up, ya blatoon hero? Your cross-eyed sergeant bush it up your ass too hard yesterday? Not strong enough to run?" He unzips his pants and takes out his dick: "What's up, Zbecial Force? My dick not good enough for you? It was blenty good for your sister, no? Blenty good for your mother, no? Blenty good for your friend Abutbul. How's he doing, Abutbul? Feeling better, boor guy? I saw they bring in a zbecial heligobter to take him away. Like a crazy man he ran after me. Half a block he ran like a majnun. Blatsh!! His face squashed up like a watermelon."

I pull up my rifle till I have him dead center in my sights.

"Go ahead and shoot, ya homo," he screams, unbuttoning his shirt and jeering. "Shoot right here." He points at his heart. I release the safety catch and hold my breath. He waits another minute or so with his arms akimbo, looking like he doesn't give a shit. His heart is deep under the skin and flesh, perfectly aligned between my sights.

"You're never going to shoot, you fucking coward. Maybe if you shoot, the cross-eyed sergeant won't go shoving it up your ass anymore, eh?"

I lower the gun, and he makes another one of his contemptuous gestures. "Yallah, I'm going, cocksucker. I'll bass by here tomorrow. When do they let you guard these barrels again? Ten till two? See you then." He starts walking off toward one of the back alleys, but suddenly he stops and smirks: "Give Abutbul regards from the Hamas, eh? Tell him we really abologize for that brick."

The rifle is back up in a flash, and I zero in till I have him right between my sights again. His shirt is buttoned up by now, but his heart is still mine. Then somebody knocks me down. I keel over in the sand, and suddenly I see Eli, the sergeant in charge. "Are you out of your mind, Meyer?" he screams. "What the hell do you think you're doing, standing there like some damn cowboy with your weapon smeared over your cheek? What do you think this is? The fucking Wild West or something, so you can go around putting slugs through anyone who comes along?"

"Dammit, Eli, I wasn't going to shoot him. I just wanted to scare him," I say, avoiding his gaze.

"You want to scare him?" he yells again, shaking me by the straps of my flak vest. "Then tell him ghost stories. What's the big idea—aiming at him with your gun cocked, and the safety off, no less?"

"Looks like Cross-Eyed isn't going to bush it up your ass today, homo," I hear the Arab shout. "Good for you, Cross-Eyed, punch him one for me too."

"You've got to learn to ignore them," Eli says, out of breath as he gets off me. "Got that, Meyer?" He switches to a menacing whisper. "You've got to learn to relax. Because if I ever see you pulling anything like this again, I'm going to see to it personally that they bring you up on charges."

That night, somebody phoned from the hospital to say that the operation hadn't gone so well, and that Abutbul would probably remain a vegetable.

"Just so long as we learn to ignore them," I spit out at Eli. "If this goes on, we'll wind up ignoring them for good, like Abutbul."

"What's your beef, Meyer?" Suddenly Eli stands up straight. "You think I don't care about Abutbul? He was as much my friend as yours, you know. You think I don't feel like taking the jeep right this minute and going from house to house and dragging them out and putting bullets through their fucking heads, every last one of them? But if I did that, I'd be just like them. Don't you get it? You don't understand anything, do you?" But suddenly I really do understand. Much better than he does.

He's standing there, in the middle of the alleyway, about twenty meters away from me, his kaffiyeh over his face.

"Good morning, Cocksucker," he yells at me. "Great morning," I whisper back.

"How's Abutbul doing, homo?" he yells at me. "Did you give him regards from the Hamas?" I let my vest fall to the ground. Then I take off my helmet.

"What's up, homo?" he shouts. "Your brain all screwed up from so much fucking with Cross-Eyed?" I tear the wrapping off my field dressing and tie it across my face like a kaffiyeh. The only thing still showing is my eyes. I take the rifle, cock it, and make sure the safety's on. I grab the butt with both hands, swing the rifle over my head a few times, and suddenly let go. It flies through the air, barely scraping the ground, then lands about midway between us. Now I'm just like him. Now I've got a chance of winning, too.

"That's for you, ya majnun," I scream at him. For

a second he just stares at me, puzzled. Then he makes a dash for the weapon. He lurches right at it, and I race toward him. He's faster than me. He'll get to it before me. But I'll win, because now I'm just like him, and with the rifle in his hand he'll be just like me. His mother and his sisters will make it with Jews, his friends will vegetate in hospital beds, and he'll stand there facing me like a fucking asshole with a rifle in his hand and won't be able to do a thing. How can I possibly lose?

He picks up the rifle, with me less than five meters away, and releases the safety lock. One knee on the ground, he aims and pulls the trigger. And then he discovers what I've discovered in this hellhole over the past month: the rifle is worth shit. Three and a half kilos of scrap metal. Totally useless. No point in even trying. I reach him before he so much as makes it up off the ground and kick him hard, right in the muzzle. As he buckles over, I drag him up by the hair and pull off his kaffiyeh. I look him in the eye. Then I grab that face and bang it against a telephone pole as hard as I can. Again and again and again. So, Sbecial Force Cocksucker, who's gonna push it up your ass now?

audience rose to its feet and applauded enthusiastically, Dad took my box of popcorn and threw it in the air, salty snowflakes landed on my head.

Some children have to run away from home in the middle of the night to join the circus, but Dad took me in his car. He and Mom helped me pack my things in a suitcase. "I'm so proud of you, son," said Dad and hugged me for a minute before I knocked on the door of Papa Luigi Santini's wagon. "Farewell, Ariel-Marcello Santini. And spare a thought for me and Mom whenever you're flying high over the circus floor."

Papa Luigi opened the door, wearing the glittering pants of his circus costume and a striped pajama top. "I want to join you, Papa Luigi," I whispered, "I want to be a flying Santini, too." Papa Luigi took a good look, felt the muscles on my thin arms with interest, and let me in. "A lot of children want to be flying Santinis," he said after a few seconds of silence. "Why do you think that you of all people are suitable?" I didn't know what to reply, so I bit my lower lip and didn't say anything. "Are you brave?" Papa Luigi asked me. I nodded. With a quick movement Papa Luigi thrust his fist in front of my face. I didn't budge, I didn't even blink. "Hmmm . . ." said Papa Luigi and stroked his chin. "And nimble?" he asked. "You know that the flying Santinis are known for their nimbleness." Again I nodded and bit hard on my lower lip. Papa Luigi held out his right hand, put a hundred-lira coin on it, and motioned to me with his silver eyebrows. I succeeded in snatching the coin before he managed to make a fist. Papa Luigi nodded, impressed. "Now there's only one test left," he thundered, "the agility test. You must touch your toes with your legs straight." I relaxed my body, took a long breath, and closed my eyes, just the way my brother Italo had done in the performance that evening. I bent over and reached with my hands. I could see the tips of my fingers just a few millimeters from my shoelaces, almost touching. My body was taut as a rope about to snap, but I didn't give up. Four millimeters separated me from the Santini family. I knew I had to cross them. And then, suddenly, I heard it. Like the sound of wood and glass breaking together, so loud it was deafening. Dad, who must have been waiting in the car outside, was alarmed by the noise and came rushing into the caravan. "Are you all right?" he asked and tried to help me up. I couldn't straighten my back. Papa Luigi lifted me in his sturdy arms, and we all drove together to the hospital.

The X ray showed a slipped disk between the L2 and L3 vertebrae. When I held it up to the light I could see a kind of black spot, like a drop of coffee, on the transparent spine. On the brown envelope they'd written "Ariel Fledermaus" with a ballpoint pen. No Marcello, no Santini—just crooked, ugly writing. "You could have bent your knees," whispered Papa Luigi and wiped one of the tears from my eyes. "You could have bent them a little. I wouldn't have said anything."

into more than smiles, and she began coming to our house, and my brother began kicking me out of the room. At first she only came for a little while, in the afternoons. Afterward she would stay for hours, and everyone in the neighborhood began to know about it. Everyone except for Korbi and his dumb friend Krotochinsky, who spent all day sitting on upturned crates outside the Persian's grocery shop, playing backgammon and drinking cherry soda. As if there were nothing else in life except those two things. They could sit at the board for hours and add up thousands of points of wins and losses that didn't interest anyone but them. When you walked past them you always had the feeling that if the Persian didn't shut the shop in the evening or if Marina didn't show up, they would be stuck there forever. Because apart from Marina, or the Persian pulling the crate out from under him, nothing would make Korbi get up.

A few months had passed since Korbi's girlfriend began visiting our house. And my brother's kicking me out of the room seemed so normal to me by then that I thought it would go on like that forever, or at least until he went to the army. Until one day my brother and I went to Youth City. It was pretty far away from our house, five miles maybe. But my brother insisted on walking instead of taking the bus, because he thought it would be a good warm-up for the Youth City ball-bouncing championship. It was

grabbed me from behind. "You," Korbi turned my brother over on his back with a few kicks, "you stole my girl when we was going steady," he yelled. His face was all red, and before my brother could reply Korbi pressed a shoe down on his neck and put almost all his weight on it. I tried to break free, but Krotochinsky's grip was too tight. "You know, Gold, there's a commandment against what you did," Korbi hissed, " 'Thou shalt not steal' is what it's called. 'Thou shalt not steal,' but you? You couldn't care less." "Thou shalt not commit adultery," I said, I don't know why. On the ground I saw my brother's eyes roll up. "What did you say?" Korbi stopped. When he turned to me a little weight was lifted from my brother's throat, and he began to cough and throw up. "I said that it was 'Thou shalt not commit adultery,' what you meant," I mumbled, "that it was a different commandment." I prayed to God that Myron would manage to get up now and that he'd beat the shit out of Korbi. "And if it was a different commandment," said Korbi, "you think that makes any difference? You think because of that I'll take my foot off your jerk-off brother's neck?" He leaned forward again. "No," I said to Korbi, "not because of that, I mean. But let go of him, Korbi, you're choking him. Can't you see he's choking?" Korbi took his foot off my brother's neck and came up to me. "Tell me, Gold, you're a good student, right? You look like a good student to me." "So-so," I mumbled. "Don't give me that so-so crap," said Korbi and touched me on the face with the back of his hand. I moved my head back. "You're a hot-shot student." Behind him, on the ground, I saw Myron trying to get up. "So you tell me, Gold," Korbi bent down and lifted the iron bar off the sidewalk, "you tell me, what was the punishment in the Bible for breaking the ten commandments?" I kept quiet. Korbi began bouncing the iron bar in his hand. "Come on, Gold," he grimaced, "tell me, so I'll know, cuz I'm thick and not such a hot-shot student like you." "I don't know," I said, "I swear on my mother. I don't know. They taught us the commandment, that's all. They didn't say anything about punishment."

Korbi turned around to my brother, who was lying on the asphalt, and gave him a kick in the ribs. Not viciously, calmly, like someone bored kicking a Coke can. A small noise came out of Myron's mouth, as if he didn't even have the strength to yell. I began to cry. "Do me a favor, Gold, don't cry," said Korbi, "just answer the question." "I don't know, motherfucker," I cried. "I don't know what the punishment is for breaking your fucking commandments. Just leave him alone, you shit, leave him alone." Krotochinsky twisted my arm behind my back with one hand and gave me a punch on the head with the other. "That's for what you said about the Bible," he spat out, "and that," he punched me again, "is for what you said about my friend." "Leave him alone, Kroto, leave him alone," said Korbi. "He's upset on account of his brother." "Please, tell me," he went on in a creaky voice while he lifted the iron bar in the air. "Tell me, or else I'll bash your brother's knee." "No, Korbi," I cried, "please don't do it." "Then tell me," said Korbi, holding the bar up, "tell me what God said somebody deserves who steals somebody else's girlfriend." "To die," I whispered, "anyone who breaks the commandment deserves to die." Korbi swung the bar right back and threw it with all his strength. It landed in the artificial lake. "Did you hear him, Kroto?" said Korbi. "Did you hear Gold Junior? He deserves to die. And I didn't say it," he pointed to the sky, "God said it." There was something in his voice, as if he was going to cry, too. "Come on," he said, "let's go. I just wanted you to hear Gold Junior say who's right." Krotochinsky let go of me and they both walked away. Before he left, Korbi touched my face again with the back of his warm hand. "You're OK, kid," he said to me, "you're OK."

In the parking lot next to the park I found someone to take us to the hospital. Compared to what it looked like, Myron got off pretty light, with an orthopedic collar for two months and a few bruises. Korbi never came near my brother again, or near Marina either. She and my brother went steady for over a year and then split up. Once, when they were still together, the whole family took a trip to the sea. Me and my brother sat on the beach and watched Marina playing in the water with my big sister. We looked at her and at the way she splashed the water with her suntanned legs, the way her long hair fell forward, almost covering her perfect face. While we were looking at her, I suddenly remembered Korbi and how he nearly cried. I asked my brother about that evening when they caught us in the park; I asked him if he still thought about it. And my brother said yes. We kept quiet for a while and watched Marina in the water. And then he said that he thought about it a lot. "Tell me," I said, "now that she's already with you, do you think that what happened then in the park was worth it?" My sister now turned her back and held up her hands to protect her head, but Marina went on splashing her and laughing. "That night," said my brother, moving his neck slowly from side to side, "nothing in the world is worth that night."

shoes

On Holocaust Memorial Day our teacher Sara took us on bus Number 57 to visit the Museum of Volhynia Jewry, and I felt very important. All the kids in the class except me, my cousin, and one other boy, Druckman, had families that came from Iraq. I was the only one with a grandfather who had died in the Holocaust. Volhynia House was very beautiful and posh, all made of black marble, like millionaires' houses. It was full of sad black-and-white pictures and lists of people and countries and dead people. We walked past the pictures in pairs and the teacher said, "Don't touch!" But I did touch one picture, made of cardboard, showing a thin, pale man who was crying and holding a sandwich in his hand. The tears came streaming down his cheeks like the divider lines you see on the highway, and my partner, Orit Salem, said she would tell the teacher that I touched it. I said I didn't care, she could tell whoever she wanted, even the principal, I didn't give a damn. It's my Grandpa and I'm touching whatever I want.

After the pictures, they took us into a big hall and showed us a movie about little children who were shoved into a truck and then suffocated with gas. Then a skinny old man got up on the stage and told us what bastards and murderers the Nazis were and how he took revenge on them, and he even strangled a soldier with his bare hands till he died. Djerby, who was sitting next to me, said the old man was lying; the way he looks, there's no way he can make any soldier bite the dust. But I looked the old man in the eye and believed him. He had so much anger in his eyes that all the rampages of all the iron-pumping hoods I'd ever seen seemed like small change in comparison.

Finally, when he finished telling us what he had done during the Holocaust, the old man said that what we had just heard was relevant not only to the past but also for what goes on nowadays, because the Germans still exist and still have a country. He said he was never going to forgive them, and that he hoped we would never ever go visit their country, either. Because when he went with his parents to Ger-

was smiling the whole time and had no idea what was going on. "They're from Germany, you know," I told her, squeezing her hand tightly. "Of course, I know," Mom smiled, "Adidas is the best brand in the world." "Grandpa was from Germany, too," I tried to give her a hint. "Grandpa was from Poland," Mom corrected me. For a moment she became sad, but she got over it in no time. She put one shoe on my foot and started to tie the laces. I kept quiet. I realized there was nothing doing. Mom didn't have a clue. She had never been to Volhynia House. Nobody had ever explained it to her. For her, shoes were just shoes and Germany was Poland. I let her put the shoes on me and didn't say a thing. There was no point in telling her and making her even sadder.

I thanked her again and kissed her on the cheek and said I was going out to play ball. "Be careful, eh?" my dad called, laughing, from his armchair in the front room. "Don't wear out the soles right away." I looked again at the pale hide covering my feet. I looked at them and remembered everything the old man who had strangled the soldier said we should remember. I touched the blue Adidas stripes and remembered my cardboard grandfather. "Are the shoes comfortable?" my mother asked. "Sure they're comfortable," my brother answered for me. "These aren't cheap Israeli sneakers. These are the same sneakers that the great Cruiff wears." I tiptoed slowly toward the door, trying to put as little weight as I could on the shoes. And so I made my way gingerly to Monkey Park. Outside, the kids from the Borochov neighborhood had formed three teams: Holland, Argentina, and Brazil. It so happened that Holland needed a player, so they agreed to let me join in, even though they never accept anyone who's not from Borochov.

At the beginning of the game I still remembered not to kick with the tip of my shoe, so that it wouldn't hurt Grandpa, but after a while I forgot, just like the old man at Volhynia House said people tend to do, and I even managed to kick a tiebreaker. But when the game was over I remembered and looked at the shoes. All of a sudden they were so comfortable, much bouncier than when they were in the box. "Some goal, eh?" I reminded Grandpa on the way home. "The goalie didn't know what hit him." Grandpa didn't answer, but judging by the tread I could tell that he was pleased, too.

that you love me," she says. What does she want me to do? What? All she has to do is tell me. But she won't. Because if I really loved her I would know by myself. What she is prepared to do is give me a clue, or say what it isn't. Either-or, I can choose. So I told her to say what it isn't; that way at least I'd know something. I wouldn't understand anything from her clues, that's for sure. "What it isn't," she says, "is anything connected to mutilating yourself, like poking out your eye or cutting off your ear, because then you'd be hurting someone I love, and indirectly you'd be hurting me, too. Hurting someone close to you is definitely not a proof of love." The truth is, I would never touch myself even if she hadn't said that. What's poking your eye out got to do with love, anyway? And what is that something? She's not prepared to say, only that doing it to my father or my brothers and sisters is no good either. I give up and tell myself that it's no use, nothing's going to do me any good. Or her either. If you insist on serving chitlins at a KKK rally, don't be surprised if you wake up with broken bones. But later on, when we're fucking and she stares deep into my eyes—she never closes her eyes when we fuck, so that I won't push somebody else's tongue in her mouth—I suddenly understand. It comes to me in a flash. "Is it my mother?" I ask, and she refuses to answer me. "If you really love me then you'll figure it out for yourself." And after she tastes the fingers she retrieves from her cunt she blurts out: "And don't bring me an ear or a finger or anything like that. It's her heart I want, you hear me? Her heart."

I traveled the whole way with the knife, two buses. A meter-and-a-half-long knife, it takes up two seats. I had to buy a ticket for it. What wouldn't I do for her, what wouldn't I do for you, baby? I walked all the way down Stampfer Avenue with the knife on my back like some would-be Islamic martyr. My mother knew I was coming, so she prepared food for me, with seasonings from hell, like only she knows how. I eat in silence; I haven't got a bad word to say. If you eat prickly pears with the thorns on, you shouldn't complain when you get piles. "And how's Miri?" asks my mother. "Is she all right, the darling girl? Still sticking her chubby fingers in her cunt?" "She's all right," I say, "she's fine. She asked for your heart. You know, so she can tell if I love her." "Take her Baruch's," my mother laughs, "she'll never notice the difference." "Come on, Mother!" I say, annoyed. "We're not into all those lies. Miri and I are into honesty." "Good," my mother sighs, "so take her mine. I don't want you to fight on my account, which reminds me, what about your proof to your mother who loves you and who you love back a little bit, too?" I slap Miri's heart down on the table in a rage. Why don't they believe me? Why are they always testing me? And now I'll have to take two buses back with this knife and my mother's heart. And she probably won't be at home, she'll go back to her ex again. Not that I'm blaming anyone, only myself.

There are two kinds of people, those who like to sleep next to the wall, and those who like to sleep next to the people who push them off the bed.

rabin's dead

Rabin's dead. It happened last night. He got run over by a scooter with a sidecar. Rabin died on the spot. The guy on the scooter got hurt real bad and passed out, and they took him away in an ambulance. They didn't even touch Rabin. He was so dead, there was nothing they could do. So me and Tiran picked him up and buried him in my backyard. I cried after that, and Tiran lit up and told me to stop crying cause I was getting on his nerves. But I didn't stop, and pretty soon he started crying too. Because I really loved Rabin a lot, but Tiran loved him even more. Then we went to Tiran's house, and there was a cop on the front stairs waiting to bag him, because the guy on the scooter came to and squealed to the doctors at the hospital. He told them Tiran had bashed his helmet in with a crowbar. The cop asked Tiran why he was crying and Tiran said, "Who's crying, you fascist motherfucking pig." The cop smacked him once, and Tiran's father came out and wanted to take down the cop's name and stuff, but the cop wouldn't tell him, and in less than five minutes, there must've been like thirty neighbors standing there. The cop told them to take it easy, and they told him to take it easy himself. There was a lot of shoving, and it looked like someone was going to get clobbered again. Finally the cop left, and Tiran's dad sat us both down in their living room and gave us some Sprite. He told Tiran to tell him what happened and to make it quick, before the cop returned with backup. So Tiran told him he'd hit someone with a crowbar but that it was someone who had it coming, and that the guy'd squealed to the police. Tiran's dad asked what exactly he had it coming for, and I could see right away that he was pissed off. So I told him it was the guy on the scooter that started it, cause first he ran Rabin over with his sidecar, then he called us names and then he went and slapped me too. Tiran's dad asked him if it was true, and Tiran didn't answer but he nodded. I could tell that he was dying for a cigarette but he was afraid to smoke next to his dad.

We found Rabin in the square. Soon as we got off

the bus we spotted him. He was just a kitten then, and he was so cold he was trembling. Me and Tiran and this uptown girl with a navel stud that we met there, we went to get him some milk. But at Espresso Bar they wouldn't give us any. And at Burger Ranch, they didn't have milk, cause they're a meat place and they're kosher, so they don't sell dairy stuff. Finally, at the grocery store on Frishman Street they gave us a half-pint and an empty yogurt cup, and we poured him some milk, and he lapped it up in one go. And Avishag—that was the name of the girl with the stud—said we ought to call him Shalom, because shalom means peace and we'd found him right in the square where Rabin died for peace. Tiran nodded and asked her for her phone number, and she told him he was really cute but that she had a boyfriend in the army. After she left, Tiran patted the kitten and said that we'd never in a million years call him Shalom, because Shalom is a sissy name. He said we'd call him Rabin, and that the broad and her boyfriend in the army could go fuck themselves for all he cared, cause maybe she had a pretty face but her body was really weird.

Tiran's dad told Tiran it was lucky he was still a minor, but even that might not do him much good this time, because bashing people with a crowbar isn't like stealing chewing gum from a candy store. Tiran still didn't say anything, and I could tell he was about to start crying again. So I told Tiran's dad that it was all my fault, because when Rabin was run over I was the one who yelled it to Tiran. And the guy on the scooter, who was kind of nice at first and even seemed sorry about what he'd done, asked me what I was screaming for. And it was only when I told him that the cat's name was Rabin that he lost his cool and slapped me. And Tiran told his dad: "First, the shit doesn't stop at the stop sign, then he runs over our cat, and after all that he goes and slaps Sinai. What did you expect me to do? Let him get away with it?" And Tiran's dad didn't answer. He lit a cigarette and without making a big deal about it lit one for Tiran too. And Tiran said the best thing I could do would be to beat it, before the cops came back, so that at least one of us would stay out of it. I told him to lay off, but his dad insisted.

Before I went upstairs, I stopped for a minute at Rabin's grave and thought about what would have happened if we hadn't found him. About what his life would have been like then. Maybe he'd have frozen to death, but probably someone else would have found him and taken him home, and then he wouldn't have been run over. Everything in life is just luck. Even the original Rabin—after everyone sang the Hymn to Peace at the big rally in the square, if instead of going down those stairs he'd hung around a little longer, he'd still be alive. And they would have shot Peres instead. At least that's what they said on TV. Or else, if the broad in the square wouldn't have had that boyfriend in the army and she'd given Tiran her phone number and we'd called Rabin Shalom, then he would have been run over anyway, but at least nobody would have got clobbered.

plague of the firstborn

In late June, after the Plague of Frogs, people began leaving the valley in droves. Those who
could afford it left a caretaker in charge of their
property, packed up their families, and set out on the
long journey to Nubia, where they intended to wait
until the wrath of the god of the Hebrews had been
spent and the plagues had run their course. One
morning, Father took Abdu and me to the King's
Highway, and together we watched in silence as the
convoy wended its way in the distance. Father was
about to head home when Abdu mustered the cour-
age to ask the question that I had not dared utter:
"Why are we not leaving with them, Father? We are
among the richest families in the valley. Why could

you not hire someone to watch over our fields so that we might also go away?" Smiling softly, Father looked at Abdu and said: "Why must we flee, Abdu? Have you too come to fear the god of the Hebrews?" "I fear no man and no god," Abdu retorted. "Whosoever challenges me I will smite with my sword! But these plagues which have been inflicted upon us come from the heavens. There are no enemies in sight for me to defy. Why then do we not join all those who are leaving for Nubia? If there are no enemies pitting their strength against ours, then our presence here avails our pharaoh nothing." "There is truth in what you say, my son," Father replied, his smile waning. "Indeed, the god of the Hebrews is both clever and cruel. Though He cannot be seen, He has dealt us a mighty blow. Yet you must understand, I am bound to this land by a vow that forbids me to send our family to Nubia." "A vow?" Abdu was taken aback. "What vow?" "A vow I made many years ago, even before you were born," Father said, his gentle smile reappearing. He gathered up his tunic and sat down on the ground, crossing his legs. "Come sit beside me," he said, patting the earth, "and I will tell you about it."

I sat down to the left of Father, and Abdu to his right. He lifted a clump of earth, crumbled it in his hands, and let the story unfold. "You know that my roots are not in this fertile soil," he began. "After your mother and I were wed, I was forced, alas, to leave her in her uncle's care and to set out with my elder brother to faraway lands, where the black oil flows from the earth. For four years we lived as nomads and endured the heartache of separation, and in those years I amassed considerable wealth. Then I returned to Egypt, to my home. I gathered up your beloved mother, who had waited for so long, and bought a plot of land here in the valley. On the very day when I completed the building of our home, I made two vows. First, never would I leave the valley. Second, I would do everything in my power so that my family does not become separated again, even for a short while." Father tasted the sand that was clinging to his palm, sat up straight, and looked into Abdu's eyes. "Even as a very young man, I knew that my family is like a plant. Uproot it, and it will wilt. Pluck away at it, and it will die. But leave it to thrive in the soil, untouched, and it will weather both gods and winds. It is born with the soil, and it will live so long as the soil shall live."

That talk with Father, far from discouraging us, made us realize how strong we were. Now we also knew the secret of that strength and guarded it zealously. With each new plague, we grew stronger still, drawing closer and closer together. When the Plague of Lice descended, we learned to delouse one another and nursed the wounds of our kinfolk. On

73

the morning after the Plague of Hail, we actually managed a smile as we watched Abdu's stupefied expression: he had just awoken out of his very deep slumber—so deep that even the hailstones rained upon us by the god of the Hebrews had not caused him to stir. Thus did the nine plagues descend on us, one by one, yet leave us unscathed. And then, toward the end of August, came the Plague of the Firstborn.

It was the shrieking of our neighbors that jolted me in the middle of the night. I ran outside and found everyone there already, except Abdu. Samira, our neighbor from just across the way, managed to blurt it out between sobs. We rushed toward Abdu's room. Father got there first, then Mother and me. Abdu was sprawled out on his cot, his eyes shut tight. "My son," Father whispered in a stifled voice, his face ashen. "My firstborn." And for the first time in my life, I saw tears in his eyes. Mine began to well with tears, too, more in agony over Father's grief than even over my brother. Seeing my sorrow through his own tears, Father wiped his eyes with the border of his tunic and drew closer to Mother and me. His powerful arms embraced us, and our faces came together. Our tears mingled and we wept as one. "The god of the Hebrews is cruel," Father resumed his whispering, as if afraid to intrude on Abdu's repose, "but he shall not defeat us."

"Could it be that he is not dead?" Mother mumbled. "That he is only sleeping?" "Please, Fatma," Father whispered and planted a gossamer kiss on her brow. "Do not leave us now for a world of delusions. Much has been said about the god of the Hebrews, but never has He been known to favor one over another. . . ." "He is not dead," Mother cried, "he cannot be dead! He is sleeping, just sleeping." She broke the stronghold of our embrace and lunged toward Abdu's cot. "Wake up, my son!" she cried, tugging at his gown. "Wake up!" Abdu opened his eyes, alarmed, and leapt out of bed. "What happened?" he asked in a daze. "It's a miracle, my son," Mother said, hugging him and gazing at Father. "A great miracle has happened."

Abdu was still! dazzled when Mother let go of him and approached Father, who was standing in a corner, his eyes to the ground. "Did you see what just happened?" she whispered. "A great miracle! The god of the Hebrews has taken pity on us, and on our son." Father peered straight ahead. His pain gave way to ill-concealed rage. "The god of the Hebrews harbors neither pity nor compassion toward us," he fumed. "Only truth. Only truth." His bloodshot eyes were like two hailstones, and his gaze filled me with greater fear than all ten plagues. "Why are you angry?" Mother asked. "Why do you not rejoice? Our Abdu is alive. . . ." "Because he is not your firstborn,"

Father cut her short. He raised his hand, as if about to strike her, but it froze in midair. Mother fell at his feet and let loose a sob as of one who has suffered an invisible blow. Thus did the four of us stand—motionless, steady, and transfixed, like a cedar about to be felled. "Cruel indeed is the god of the Hebrews," Father said. Then he turned on his heel and left the room.

siren

On Holocaust Remembrance Day there was an assembly in the auditorium. A makeshift stage had been put up, and on the wall behind it they had stuck up sheets of black cartridge paper with the names of concentration camps and pictures of barbed-wire fences. As we filed in, Shelley asked me to save her a seat, so I grabbed two. She sat down next to me and it was a little crowded on the bench. I put my elbow on my knee and the back of my hand brushed against her jeans. They were thin and nice to touch, and I felt as if I'd touched her body.

"Where's Mikey?" I asked. "I haven't seen him today." My voice was a little shaky.

"He's doing the naval commando tests," Shelley

replied proudly. "He's already passed almost all the stages, he just has one more interview to do."

At the other side of the hall I saw Ron coming toward us down the aisle. Shelley went on. "Did you hear that he's going to get the Outstanding Student Award at the graduation party? The principal has already announced it."

"Shelley," called Ron, who came up to us, "what are you doing here? These benches aren't comfortable. Come on, I saved you a seat at the back."

"OK," Shelley said, giving me an apologetic smile and getting up. "It's really crowded here."

She went to sit with Ron at the back. Ron was Mikey's best friend, they played together on the school basketball team. I looked at the stage and took a deep breath. My hand was still sweating. Some of the ninth-graders got up on the stage and the ceremony began.

When all of the students had finished rattling off the usual texts, an old-looking old man in a maroon sweater came onto the stage and told us about Auschwitz. He was the father of one of the kids. He didn't speak long, just fifteen minutes or so. Afterward we went back to class. As we went out I saw Sholem, our janitor, sitting on the steps by the nurse's room, crying.

"Hey, Sholem, what's wrong?" I asked.

"That man in the hall," he said, "I know him, I was in the *Sonderkommando* too."

"You were in the commandos? When?" I asked. I couldn't picture our skinny old Sholem in any kind of commando unit, but you never know.

Sholem wiped his eyes with the back of his hand and stood up. "Never mind," he said. "Go, go back to class. It doesn't matter."

I went down to the shopping center in the afternoon. At the falafel stall I met Benny and Josh. "Guess what," Josh said, with his mouth full of falafel, "Mikey passed the interview today, then he'll have one little orientation course and he's in the naval commandos. You know what that means? They're handpicked. . . ."

Benny began swearing. His pita split open and all the tahina and the juices from the salad were dripping over his hands. "We just saw him on the basketball court. Ron and him were celebrating, with beer and everything."

Josh giggled and choked, and bits of tomato and pita went flying out of his mouth. "You should have seen them joyriding on Sholem's bike, like little kids. Mikey was so stoked at passing the interview. My brother said the interview is where they eliminate the most candidates."

I walked over to the school but there was no one

there. Sholem's bike, which was always chained to the railing by the nurse's office, was gone. On the steps there was a chain and a padlock. When I got to school the next morning the bike still wasn't there. I waited for everyone to go into class and then I went to tell the principal. He told me I'd done the right thing and that no one would know about our talk, and he asked the secretary to give me a late pass. Nothing happened that day or the day after, but on Thursday the principal came into our classroom with a cop in uniform and asked Mikey and Ron to step outside.

The police didn't do anything to them, just cautioned them. They couldn't give back the bike because they'd just dumped it somewhere, but Mikey's father came to school specially and brought Sholem a new mountain bike. At first, Sholem didn't want to accept it. "Walking is healthier," he said to Mikey's dad. But Mikey's dad insisted, and in the end Sholem took the bike. It was funny seeing Sholem riding a mountain bike, and I knew that the principal was right and I'd done the right thing. No one suspected that I'd told on them, at least that's what I thought at the time. The next two days went by as usual, but when I came to school on Monday, Shelley was waiting for me in the yard. "Listen, Eli," she said, "Mikey found out you were the one that snitched about the bike; you've got to get out of here before him and Ron get hold of you."

I tried to hide my fear; I didn't want Shelley to see I was scared.

"Quick, beat it," she said.

I started to walk away.

"No, not through there," she said, pulling my arm. The touch of her hand was cool and pleasant. "They'll be coming through the gate, so you'd better go through the hole in the fence behind the sheds."

Even more than I was scared, I was glad that Shelley was that worried about me.

Mikey was waiting for me behind the sheds. "Don't even think about it," he said, "you haven't got a chance."

I turned around. Ron was standing behind me.

"I always knew you were a worm," said Mikey, "but I never thought you were a rat."

"Why did you squeal on us, you piece of shit?" Ron said and gave me a strong shove. I stumbled into Mikey and he pushed me away.

"I'll tell you why he squealed," Mikey said. "Because our Eli is jealous as hell. He looks at me and sees that I'm a better student than him, a better athlete, and I've got a girlfriend who's the prettiest girl in school, while he's still a poor virgin, and it eats him up."

Mikey took off his leather jacket and handed it to Ron. "OK, Eli, you did it, you screwed me," he said, unfastening the strap of his diver's watch and putting it in his pocket. "My dad thinks I'm a thief, the police almost charged me. I won't get the Outstanding Student Award. Are you happy now?"

I wanted to tell him it wasn't that, it was because of Sholem who was also in a commando unit, because he cried like a baby on Holocaust Day. Instead I said, "You shouldn't have stolen his bike, it didn't make sense. You have no honor." My voice shook as I spoke.

"You hear that, Ron, this whining rat is telling us about honor. Honor is not snitching on your friends, you shit," he said, balling his fist. "Now Ron and me are going to teach you all about honor, the hard way."

I wanted to get away from there, to run, to raise my hands and protect my face, but the fear paralyzed me. Then suddenly, out of nowhere, there came the wail of the memorial siren. I'd completely forgotten that it was Remembrance Day for the fallen soldiers. Mikey and Ron came to attention. I looked at them standing there like shop-window mannequins and suddenly I wasn't afraid anymore. Ron, standing rigidly to attention, eyes closed, holding Mikey's jacket, looked like an oversized coat hanger. And Mikey, with his murderous look and clenched fists, suddenly looked like a little boy imitating a pose he'd seen in an action movie. I walked to the hole in the fence and passed through it, slowly and quietly, while behind me I heard Mikey hiss, "We're still going to fuck you," but he didn't budge. I walked on home through the streets with all the frozen people looking like wax dummies. The sound of the siren protected me with an invisible shield.

fed us, and if anyone so much as opened his mouth, they let us have it with a belt. Lots of times they'd give you the belt without bothering to open the buckle. When Grace arrived, they made sure to get us cleaned up—us and that shithole they called an orphanage. Before he came in, the director gave us a briefing: anyone who blabbered would be in for it later. We'd all had our share of his medicine, enough to know he meant business. When Grace entered our rooms, we were silent as mice. He tried talking with us, but we didn't really answer. Each boy got his present, said thank-you, and hurried back into bed. I got a dartboard. When I said thank-you, he reached for my face. I cringed. Thought he was going to hit me. Grace ran his hand over my hair, gently, and without a word he lifted my shirt. In those days I used to shoot off my mouth a lot. Grace could figure that out by the look of my back. He didn't say anything at first. Then he said the name of Jesus a few times. Finally, he let go of my shirt and hugged me. While he was hugging me, he promised that nobody would ever hit me again. Needless to say, I didn't believe him. People don't just act nice to you for no good reason. I figured it had to be some kind of a trick; he'd be slipping off his belt any minute and letting me have it. The whole time he was hugging me, I just wanted him to go. He went, and that same evening we got a new director and a whole new staff. From that time on, nobody ever hit me again, except that nigger I wiped out in Jacksonville. Did that one pro bono. Since then, nobody's lifted a finger on me.

I never saw Patrick Grace again. But I read about him in the papers a lot. About all the people he'd helped, all the good things he did. He was a good man. I guess there was no finer man anywhere. The only man I owed a favor on the whole face of this ugly planet. And in two hours I'm supposed to be meeting him. In two hours I'm supposed to be putting a bullet through his head.

I'm thirty-one. I've had twenty-nine contracts since I got started. Twenty-six of them I completed in one go. I never try to understand the people I kill. Never try to understand why. Business is business, and like I said, I'm a pro. I've got a good reputation, and in a profession like mine a good reputation is all that counts. You don't exactly place an ad in the paper or offer special rates to people with the right credit card. The only thing that keeps you in business is that people know they can count on you to get the job done. That's why I've made it a policy never to back out on a contract. Anyone who checks my record will find nothing but satisfied customers. Satisfied customers and stiffs.

I rented a room facing the street, right opposite the café. Told the owner that the rest of my belongings would be arriving on Monday and paid two months' rent up front. There was half an hour to kill till the time I figured he'd get there. I assembled the gun and zeroed in the infrared sight. Only twenty-six minutes left. I lit a cigarette. I was trying not to think about anything. Finished the cigarette and flicked what was left of it into the corner of the room. Who'd want to kill a person like that? Only an animal or a complete wacko. I know Grace. He hugged me when I was just a kid. But business is business. Once you let your feelings in you're through. The carpet in the corner began to smolder. I got up off the bed and stepped on the butt. Another eighteen minutes. Another eighteen minutes and it would be over. I tried thinking about football, about Dan Marino, about a hooker on Forty-second Street who gives me head in the front seat of the car. I tried not to think about anything.

He was right on time. I recognized him from behind by that special bouncy walk of his and the shoulder-length hair. He took a seat at one of the tables outside, in the best-lit spot, so that he was facing me head-on. The angle was perfect. Medium range. I could take this shot blindfolded. The red dot showed on the side of his head, a little too far to the left. I corrected to the right till it was dead center and held my breath.

Just when I had it all set, an old man wandered by, carrying all his earthly possessions in a couple of

the table and told him that someone had hired me to kill him. I tried to play it cool, to pretend like I'd never even considered going through with it. Grace smiled and said that he knew. That he was the one who'd sent the money in the envelope, that he wanted to die. I've got to admit his answer caught me off-guard. I stammered. Asked why. Did he have some malignant disease? "A disease?" he laughed. "Guess you could say that." There was that little spasm again at the corner of his mouth, the one I'd seen through the window, and he started to talk: "Ever since I was a kid I've had this disease. The symptoms were clear, but nobody ever tried treating it. I'd give my toys to the other kids. I never lied. I never stole. I was never even tempted to hit back in school fights. I was always sure to turn the other cheek. My compulsive good-heartedness just got worse over the years, but nobody was willing to do anything about it. If, say, I'd been compulsively bad, they'd have taken me to a shrink or something right away. They'd have tried to stop it. But when you're good? It suits people in our society to keep getting what they need in return for a shriek of delight and a few compliments. And I just kept getting worse. It's reached the point where I can't even eat without stopping after every bite to find someone who's hungrier to finish my meal. And at night, I can't fall asleep. How can a person even consider sleeping when you live in New York and sixty feet away from your house people are shivering on a park bench."

The spasm was back at the corner of his mouth, and his whole body shook. "I can't go on this way, with no sleep, no food, no love. Who has time for love when there's so much misery around? It's a nightmare. Try to see it from my point of view. I never asked to be this way. It's like a dybbuk. Except that instead of a dybbuk, your body is possessed by an angel. Damn it. If it were a devil, someone would have tried to finish me off a long time ago. But this?" Grace gave a short sigh and closed his eyes. "Listen," he went on. "All this money, take it. Go find yourself a position on some balcony or rooftop and get it over with. I can't do it on my own, after all. And it gets harder every day. Even just sending you the money, having this conversation," he mopped his forehead, "it's hard. Very hard on me. I'm not sure I'll have what it takes to do it again. Please, just pick a spot up on one of the rooftops and do it. I'm begging you." I looked at him. At his tormented face. Like Jesus on the cross, just like Jesus. I didn't say anything. Didn't know what to say. I'm always armed with the right sentence, whether it's for the father confessor, for a hooker in a bar, or for a federal agent. But with him? With him I was a scared little kid again at the orphanage, cringing at every unexpected move. And he was a good man, *the* good man,

I'd never be able to waste him. No point even trying. My finger just wouldn't wrap itself around the trigger.

"Sorry, Mr. Grace," I whispered after a long while. "I just . . ."

"You just can't kill me," he smiled. "That's OK. You're not the first, you know. Two other guys have returned the envelope before you. I guess it's part of the curse. It's just that you, with the orphanage and all . . ." He shrugged. "And me getting weaker every day. Somehow I'd hoped you could return the favor."

"Sorry, Mr. Grace," I whispered. I had tears in my eyes. "I wish I could . . ."

"Don't feel bad," he said. "I understand. No harm done. Leave it," he chuckled when he saw me pick up the tab. "Coffee's on me. I insist. It has to be on me, you know. It's like a disease." I pushed the crumpled bill back in my pocket. Then I thanked him and walked away. After I'd taken a few steps, he called me. I'd forgotten the gun.

I went back to get it, cussing quietly to myself. Felt like a rookie.

Three days later, in Dallas, I shot some senator. It was a tricky one. From two hundred yards away, half a view, side wind. He was dead before he hit the floor.

katzenstein

In Hell, they put me in a cauldron of boiling water. My flesh smoldered and burned, my skin was covered with blisters, and the pain was so bad I couldn't stop screaming. They had these giant screens where you could see everything that was going on in Heaven. Suffer and eat your heart out, watch the screen and suffer. I think I spotted him there for a second, playing golf or cricket or something. There was a kind of close-up of his smile, and right after that they showed this couple making love.

Once, after we'd made love, my wife said: "Seven years you've been with them, slaving for them, bringing work home every weekend, and now, when push comes to shove, they won't give you a promotion.

And you know why? Because you don't know how to sell yourself, that's why. Take Katzenstein for example." I took Katzenstein for example. My whole life I'd been taking Katzenstein for example. I wanted to take a shower, but there was no hot water. The water heater was broken. Took a cold shower instead. I bet Katzenstein has a solar heater.

In high school, I couldn't get into honors class. To my mother it was a really big deal. She cried her eyes out and said I'd never amount to anything. I tried to tell her how tough it was to get in, that only ten percent made it, only the really smart kids. "I met Miriam Katzenstein at the grocery store today," Mom sighed. "Her son got in. Is Miriam Katzenstein's son smarter than mine? Not on your life! He just tries harder. And you—it's as if you're trying to spite me. Driving me to an early grave."

Wherever I went he was always there for them to compare me to. In class, on the block, in the yard, at work, everywhere. Katzenstein, Katzenstein, Katzenstein, Katzenstein. It's not that he was a prodigy or anything. An average guy, no genius, no great shakes at athletics and not very sharp either. Just like me, only a tiny bit better. A tiny bit here and a tiny bit there and another tiny bit . . . hell.

It was my own idea to quit my job. It cost me plenty of fights with my wife, but eventually she resigned herself to it. We moved to a different city, far away, and I started working as an insurance salesman. Did pretty well. Didn't see him for about seven years. Things were going my way. My son was born. My grandfather in Switzerland died and left me a lot of property. On the flight back from Basel I saw him sitting there, in first class. By the time I spotted him it was too late. The plane was taxiing down the runway, and I knew I was in for five very long hours. Next to me was this rabbi who didn't stop yapping, but I didn't hear a word. For five hours straight, my eyes were glued to the back of Katzenstein's head. "Take a good look at the empty life you lead. You're a shell of a man. No values." The rabbi was holding a mirror up to my sins, sprinkling his sermon with sacred verses. I had some orange juice. Katzenstein ordered a Jack Daniel's. "For example, take . . ." the rabbi said. No thanks. I sprang up and made a dash for the rear of the plane. The flight attendant asked me to return to my seat. I wouldn't.

"We're about to land, sir. I insist you return to your seat and fasten your seatbelt, like . . ." True, she went on to say "like all the other passengers," but what I saw in her eyes was Katzenstein. I pushed down on the lever and forced the door open with my shoulder. I was perfectly calm as I was sucked out, leaving all hell behind me.

Suicide is still considered a dreadful sin in the afterlife. I begged them to try and understand, but they wouldn't listen. As they were dragging me to Hell, there was Katzenstein. Him and the other passengers, waving at me through the window of the tour bus that was taking them to Heaven. The plane had crashed as it hit the ground, about fifteen minutes after I'd bailed out. A rare malfunction. One in a million. If only I'd stuck it out in my seat another few seconds, like all the other passengers. Like Katzenstein.

the mysterious
disappearance of alon
shemesh

On Tuesday Alon Shemesh didn't show up at school, and when the teacher, Miss Nava, handed out the stencils, she gave Jakie two of them, because he's Alon Shemesh's best friend, and their families know each other, and they go on picnics together on the weekend and everything, so it made the most sense for Jakie to bring Alon his homework. "And Jacob, don't forget to wish Alon a speedy recovery from the entire class," she announced. Jakie, who's a regular con artist, went like, "Piss off, you bitch," with his head, but the teacher thought it was just a nod.

Wednesday morning Jakie didn't show up at school either. "He must have caught it," wheezed Aviva Krantenstein the crammer. Meyer Subban wasn't buying: "No way. I bet they're both playing hooky, together with their families," he said. "They're all having a cookout on the beach." "Quiet, children," Miss Nava squeaked. "Do we have any volunteers to bring the homework to the children who are home sick?" "I'll take it to Alon," Yuval volunteered. "We live on the same block." "And I'll take it to Jacob," Dikla snapped before anyone else got a chance. Everyone knows she has the hots for Jakie. "And I'll take it to Jacob," Meyer Subban mimicked, and everybody laughed. "Wanting to help a sick friend is nothing to make fun of. I will call the children who are not well myself, to see how they are." "Wanting to help, my foot. She's itching to get laid, that one," Gafni said in a really loud whisper and was out on his ass.

The next day Yuval and Dikla didn't show up either. "I don't know about the others," Subban said, "but Yuval stayed home because of the geography test. I'll bet you anything." "Maybe they came down with typhoid fever. It says in the reader that the pioneers had it a lot. . . ." Aviva Krantenstein was at it again, but Gafni threatened to burn every notebook she owned, so she shut her trap. "I tried calling the homes of the children who are absent, but there was no answer," Miss Nava said. "I have no choice but to pay them a visit. And meanwhile, I forbid you to visit the absentees until I make certain that they are not contagious."

After school the whole class met by the mulberry tree at King David Park. "Who does she think she is, telling us we can't visit our own friends?" Meyer Subban yelled. "Thinks she's hot shit," Gafni was getting worked up too. "We'll show her! We're all going to visit Jakie today. And no excuses, Krantenstein. So help me, if I don't see you there, I'm going to swallow every fucking magic marker you've got."

I couldn't go in the end. My mother left me a note saying the repairman was coming to fix the fridge and that she'd be late, so I had to stay home, which really pissed me off. I knew Gafni would believe me, but some of the others would say I was chicken.

Friday, just me and Michel de Casablanca showed up at school. Not even the teacher came. Michel de Casablanca said nobody told him yesterday about the meeting at King David Park, so he just went home. We put the wastepaper basket on the desk and shot spitballs all morning.

It's been a week, and Michel and me are really cool now. He's been teaching me all kinds of games with funny French names, and we're having a swell time. Mom says it's outrageous, what's going on at school, and she wants to get the parents together, but except at Michel's place there's no answer at anyone's house, and she can't get hold of the principal either. His secretary says he called three days ago to tell her he'd be a little late because he was stopping to visit Miss Nava, and he hasn't been heard from since. Mom is taking the whole thing very hard. Keeps chain-smoking and writing letters to the ministry of education. "Don't worry, Miss Abadda," Michel keeps trying to reassure her. "They probably all went for a cookout on the beach." He may be right, I don't know anymore. Or maybe Aviva Krantenstein knew what she was talking about and they really did all die of typhoid fever.

get there, remove the soul, undo the Velcro, pull out the talent, and that's that. The guy can kick and scream till the cows come home. You're the daemon. You check them off and keep going down the list. But the nice ones, the ones that talk real softly, with the truffles and the lemonades and all—what can you say to them? "OK," the daemon sighed, "one last one. But make it short, eh? It's almost three, and I've got at least two more stops today." "Short," the guy gave a tired smile, "very short, even. Four pages tops. You can watch TV in the meantime."

After tucking away two more truffles, the daemon stretched out on the sofa and started fiddling with the remote. Meanwhile, in the other room, the guy who'd given him the truffles was clicking away at the keyboard at a nice even pace, never letting up, like somebody keying a million-digit PIN into an ATM. "I hope he turns out something really good," the daemon thought to himself and stared at an ant plodding across the screen in a nature film on PBS. "The kind with lots of trees and a little girl who's looking for her parents. Something with a beginning that grabs you by the nuts and an ending that's so heartwrenching, people get all choked up." He really was a nice person, that guy. Not just nice, he was dignified. And the daemon was hoping, for the guy's sake, that he was just about done. It was after four, and in twenty minutes, half an hour tops, finished or not, he'd have to undo the guy's Velcro, pull out the stuff, and split. Otherwise they'd give him such shit in the stockroom later, he'd rather not even think about it.

But the guy was good as his word. Five minutes later he came out of the other room all sweaty, with four printed pages in his hand. The story he wrote was really good. Not about a little girl, and not one that grabs you by the nuts, but moving as hell. And when the daemon told him so, the guy was pretty psyched, and it showed. And that smile of his lingered on, even after the daemon pulled out his talent, folded it up very very small, and put it in a special box lined with Styrofoam peanuts. And all that time the guy didn't give him the tormented-artist look even once. Just kept offering him more truffles. "Tell your bosses thanks," he told the daemon. "Tell them I had a helluva time with it, the talent and everything. Don't forget." And the daemon told him fine and thought to himself that if instead of a daemon he'd been human, or if only they'd met under different circumstances, they could have been cool together. "Any idea what you'll do now?" the daemon asked, concerned, standing in the doorway by then. "Not really. Guess I'll get to go to the beach more often, see my friends, that kind of thing. And you?" "Work," the daemon said and adjusted the box on his back. "Me, apart from work, there's nothing on my mind. Believe me." "Say," the guy asked, "just out of curiosity, what do they do in the end with all those talents?" "I don't actually know," the daemon admitted. "My job's just as far as the stockroom. That's where they count 'em up, sign my delivery slips, and that's it. What happens with them later—I haven't the faintest." "If you wind up with one too many, I'll always be glad to take it back," the guy laughed and tapped on the box. And the daemon laughed too, but it was a kind of fed-up laugh. And the whole four floors down all he could think about was the story the guy had written, and this pickup job, which he used to sort of enjoy but now suddenly seemed like such a crock of shit. "Two more stops," he tried to console himself on his way to the car. "Just a lousy two more stops and I'm done for the day."

jetlag

On my last flight home from New York a flight attendant fell in love with me. I know what you're thinking—that I'm a show-off or a liar or both. That I think I'm some kind of a hunk or at least that I want you to think so. But I don't. And she really did fall in love with me. It began right after takeoff, when the drinks were being served. When I said I didn't want anything and she insisted on pouring me some tomato juice.

Truth is, I was getting suspicious even before that, during the emergency drill before takeoff, when she didn't take her eyes off me, as if the whole thing was just for me.

And if that wasn't enough, she brought me

another roll after dinner, as soon as I'd finished eating. "There was only one left," she told the little girl sitting next to me, who was giving the roll a hungry look, "and the gentleman asked for it first." But I hadn't. To cut a long story short, she had the hots for me. The little girl had noticed it too. "She's got it bad for you," she said when her mother or whoever she was went to the toilet.

"Go for it, go for it right now. Give it to her right here on the plane, with her leaning on the duty-free cart just like Sylvia Kristel in *Emmanuelle*. Go ahead, screw her, brother, bang the hell out of her, for my sake too." It surprised me a little, that kind of talk coming from a little girl. She seemed like this well-behaved, barely ten-year-old blond little thing, and suddenly all this "bang her" and *Emmanuelle* stuff. It was embarrassing, so I tried to change the subject.

"First time you're going abroad, sweetie?" I asked. "Mommy taking you on a trip?"

"She's not my mother," she spat back. "And I'm not a little girl. I'm a dwarf in disguise, and she's my operator. And keep this under your hat, but the only reason I'm wearing this getup is because I'm walking around with five pounds of heroin stuck up my ass." After that, the mother came back and the little girl started acting normal again, except whenever the flight attendant passed by with cups of water and peanuts and the things that flight attendants bring, smiling, mostly at me.

That's when the little girl would wake up and make these really vulgar screwing gestures. After a while she got up to go to the toilet, and her mother, who was in the aisle seat, gave me a tired smile. "She probably drove you bonkers while I was gone," she shook her head sadly. "I guess she told you I'm not really her mother, and that she used to be a marine commander, and stuff like that." I shook my head, but she went on. You could tell she was carrying the whole world on her shoulders and that she was dying to share it with somebody.

"Ever since her father died, she's been trying to punish me," she began. "As if I was to blame for his death." By now she was really crying. "It's not your fault, ma'am," I said, placing a comforting hand on her shoulder. "Nobody thinks you're to blame." "And how they do!" she snapped, pushing my hand away. "I know they do, but the fact is that I was acquitted in a court of law, so don't you patronize me. Who knows what awful things you have lurking in your past!"

The little girl was coming back. She glared at her mother to shut her up. Then she gave me a softer look. I was huddled in my seat by the window, trying to remember what awful things were lurking in my past, when I felt a small, sweaty hand pushing a crumpled piece of paper into my hand. "My love," it said. "Please meet me in the kitchenette." It was signed THE FLIGHT ATTENDANT in large, childish block letters.

The little girl winked at me. I stayed put. Every few minutes she'd elbow me, till finally I'd had enough. So I got out of my seat and pretended to be heading for the kitchenette. I was going to walk toward the tail, count to a hundred, and head back. I hoped maybe by then the little pest would lay off. There was less than an hour left to the flight. God knows I was dying to get home. Near the toilet, I heard someone calling me in a soft voice. It was the flight attendant.

"Good thing you came right away," she said, kissing me on the mouth. "I was afraid that creepy kid wouldn't give you the note." I tried to say something, but she was kissing me again. Then she pulled away. "There's no time to lose," she panted. "The plane's about to crash any minute now. I've got to save you." "Crash?" I jumped. "But why? What's wrong?" "Nothing's wrong," Shelley said, shaking her head. I could tell her name was Shelley, because that's what her tag said.

"We're going to crash on purpose." "Who's we?" I asked. "The flight crew," she said without batting an eye. "It's an order from the top. Once every year or two we crash a plane in mid-ocean, as gently as possible, and a child or two may get killed, so people start taking the whole flight safety business more seriously. You know, so they'll pay attention when we give those demonstrations of emergency procedures and all that." "But why this plane?" I asked. She shrugged. "Dunno. It's an order from the top. Probably they caught on that things were getting a little sloppy lately."

"But . . ." I tried. "Where are the emergency exits?" she fired at me without letting me finish the sentence. To be honest, I couldn't remember. "You see," she nodded her head. "People are too complacent. Don't worry, my love. Most of them will survive, but with you, I just couldn't risk it." Then she bent over and handed me this plastic backpack, like a kid's schoolbag. "What's this?" I asked. "A parachute," she kissed me again. "At the count of three, I'll open the door. That's when you jump. Actually, you won't even need to jump, you'll be sucked out."

To be perfectly honest, I didn't really want to. Jumping out of airplanes in the middle of the night just isn't my thing. Shelley thought I was worried about her, afraid of getting her in trouble. "Don't worry," she said, "if you don't tell anyone, no one will ever find out. You can always tell them you swam your way to Greece."

I don't really remember anything about the jump, only the waters below, cold as a polar bear's ass. I tried to swim a little, but then I realized I could stand. So I started wading toward the lights. My head was throbbing, and the fishermen on shore were getting on my nerves, making out like I'd been in deep trouble and they'd saved me, just so I'd give them a few bucks—carried me on their backs, mouth-to-mouth resuscitation, the works. But when they tried a body rub, I really lost it and slapped one of them.

I'd obviously hurt their feelings, and they left. Next, I checked into the Holiday Inn, but I couldn't fall asleep, on account of the jetlag, I guess, so I watched cable. On CNN they were showing the rescue operation live, which was kind of exciting. I recognized lots of people from the line to the toilet. They were being scooped into lifeboats and were all smiling and waving at the cameras. On TV it looked really heartwarming, the whole rescue operation.

It turned out there'd been no casualties except for one little girl, and even she turned out to be a dwarf who'd been wanted by Interpol, so that all in all, things had turned our pretty well. I got out of bed and walked to the bathroom. From a distance I could still hear the cheerful off-key singing of the survivors. And just for a second, from the depths of the bidet in my sad hotel room, I could imagine myself there with the rest of them, hugging my Shelley on the bottom of the lifeboat and refusing to wave at the cameras.

And there was that name of his, Oleg. He seemed such an unlikely candidate for son of the Head of the Mossad that sometimes you couldn't help asking yourself whether it wasn't just another stunt that his father, the Head of the Mossad, had thought up to disguise his true identity.

There were days when the Head of the Mossad didn't leave the house. Other days he'd get home very late. On those days, when he'd get home he'd give a tired smile to the son of the Head of the Mossad and to his mother and say: "What a day I had, don't ask." And they didn't, they just went on watching TV or doing homework. Even if they had asked him, he wouldn't have answered anyway.

The son of the Head of the Mossad had a girlfriend. Her name was Gabi. They'd talk together about everything. He and Gabi did most of their talking lying on the floor in his room. They'd form a T, with Gabi's head on the stomach of the son of the Head of the Mossad. Gabi's mother died when she was a baby, but she told Oleg that she could actually remember being breast-fed. The son of the Head of the Mossad said that his earliest memory was when he was about two and a half. They were in the car, and someone was honking like crazy behind them, and his dad was at the wheel, serene as a Buddha. "They can honk till hell freezes over, for all I care, Aviva," he said in his serene voice. "They'll give up in the end," and "He can cry till hell freezes over too, for all I care. He'll give up in the end too." Gabi used to have a different boyfriend, Simon. Simon had been in their class in high school, but they threw him out at the beginning of eleventh grade and he went to work for his dad, because he'd thrown a brick at Sylvia, the vice-principal. Simon's father was an earth-mover too, and he couldn't stand the Head of the Mossad. "Everyone's always talking about the contracts his company won," he told Simon once, "but I've never once seen him on a bulldozer, getting a single project off the ground." Simon and his dad thought there was something fishy going on, like the company of the Head of the Mossad was getting paid by the government for work it wasn't really doing. A thought that certainly had a leg to stand on. And if you add the fact that the son of the Head of the Mossad stole Simon's girlfriend from him, it's pretty easy to understand why Simon hated the son of the Head of the Mossad in the worst possible way.

Once, the son of the Head of the Mossad was playing basketball at the sports center. He went there with his friend Ehud. Ehud was tall and strong and was always quiet. Lots of people thought Ehud was quiet because he was stupid. That wasn't true. He may not have been the smartest kid on the block, but he was no moron either. In some ways, Ehud was better suited to be the son of the Head of the Mossad than his real son was. His coolheadedness and his inner calm were just two of the qualities that made him the ideal candidate. And sure enough, the Head of the Mossad liked Ehud a lot. Whenever Ehud came over, the Head of the Mossad would give him a man-to-man slap on the back and say: "What's up, big guy?" And Ehud would smile and keep quiet. It was really out of character. The Head of the Mossad never gave the son of the Head of the Mossad a slap on the back, for example. He never gave a slap on the back to anyone except Ehud and the deputy chief of intelligence, and even then it was only because the two of them had been in officers' training together and had saved each other's lives a dozen times. When it started getting dark they stopped playing, and the son of the Head of the Mossad headed home. Ehud stayed behind on the court after everyone had left so that he could practice shooting baskets, as usual.

The son of the Head of the Mossad walked through the playground and looked at the old swings and ladders. There was nobody there, because it was already getting dark. Nobody except Simon, who was sitting on the edge of the sandbox, looking like he'd had too much to drink. Simon was very down that night, partly because he'd wrecked one of his dad's bulldozers, but mainly because he'd discovered that his sister was fucking one of the Arab workers. He'd

about the blade, and about Simon. His dad asked if Simon had actually touched him at any point, and whether he had tried to stand his ground, and whether Ehud had stripped too, because the son of the Head of the Mossad forgot to tell him that Ehud had stayed behind on the court to keep practicing. When he'd finished the interrogation, the Head of the Mossad said: "OK, you can go get dressed," and he sat down at his desk, fuming. The son of the Head of the Mossad got into bed naked, pulled the blanket over his head, and started to cry. His mother, who had just stood there the whole time his father was interrogating him and hadn't said a word, came in and hugged him till he stopped crying, and she thought he was asleep. After that, for the first time in his life, he heard his father yelling in the living room. Only some of the words reached him through the blanket, like "your fault," "not even a scratch," "no—I'm not overreacting," and "Ehud, for one."

The next morning, the Head of the Mossad checked the clip and put the gun back in the drawer. Then he gave his son a ride to school. They didn't say a word the whole way, as usual. At two o'clock, the son of the Head of the Mossad finished lunch and said he was going out to play basketball. That night, when the son of the Head of the Mossad came home, he gave his father and mother a tired smile and said, "What a day I had, don't ask." And they didn't. Later, when his father went to the bathroom and his mother was already asleep, he put the gun back in the bottom drawer. Even if they had asked him, he wouldn't have answered anyway.

disorders" and had me transferred to carpentry school. When I got there, it turned out I was allergic to sawdust, so they transferred me to metalworking class. I was pretty good at it, but I didn't really enjoy it. To tell the truth, I didn't really enjoy anything in particular. When I finished school, I started working in a factory that made pipes. My boss was an engineer with a diploma from a top technical college. A brilliant guy. If you showed him a picture of a kid without ears or something like that, he'd figure it out in no time.

After work I'd stay on at the factory and make myself odd-shaped pipes, winding ones that looked like curled-up snakes, and I'd roll marbles through them. I know it sounds like a dumb thing to do, and I didn't even enjoy it, but I went on doing it anyway.

One night I made a pipe that was really complicated, with lots of twists and turns in it, and when I rolled a marble in, it didn't come out at the other end. At first I thought it was just stuck in the middle, but after I tried it with about twenty more marbles, I realized they were simply disappearing. I know that everything I say sounds kind of stupid. I mean everyone knows that marbles don't just disappear, but when I saw the marbles go in at one end of the pipe and not come out at the other end, it didn't even strike me as strange. It seemed perfectly OK, actually. That was when I decided to make myself a bigger pipe, in the same shape, and to crawl into it until I disappeared. When the idea came to me, I was so happy that I started laughing out loud. I think it was the first time in my entire life that I laughed.

From that day on, I worked on my giant pipe. Every evening I'd work on it, and in the morning I'd hide the parts in the storeroom. It took me twenty days to finish making it. On the last night it took me five hours to assemble it, and it took up about half the shop floor.

When I saw it all in one piece, waiting for me, I remembered my social studies teacher who said once that the first human being to use a club wasn't the strongest person in his tribe or the smartest. They didn't need a club, while he did. He needed a club more than anyone, to survive and to make up for being weak. I don't think there was a human being in the whole world who wanted to disappear more than I did, and that's why it was me that invented the pipe. Me, and not that brilliant engineer with his technical college degree who runs the factory.

I started crawling inside the pipe, with no idea about what to expect at the other end. Maybe there would be kids there without ears, sitting on mounds of marbles. Could be. I don't know exactly what happened after I passed a certain point in the pipe. All I know is that I'm here.

I think I'm an angel now. I mean, I've got wings

and this circle over my head and there are hundreds more here like me. When I got here they were sitting around playing with the marbles I'd rolled through the pipe a few weeks earlier.

I always used to think that Heaven is a place for people who've spent their whole lives being good, but it isn't. God is too merciful and kind to make a decision like that. Heaven is simply a place for people who were genuinely unable to be happy on earth. They told me here that people who kill themselves return to live their life all over again, because the fact that they didn't like it the first time doesn't mean they won't fit in the second time. But the ones who really don't fit in the world wind up here. They each have their own way of getting to Heaven.

There are pilots who got here by performing a loop at one precise point in the Bermuda Triangle. There are housewives who went through the back of their kitchen cabinets to get here, and mathematicians who found topological distortions in space and had to squeeze through them to get here. So if you're really unhappy down there, and if all kinds of people are telling you that you're suffering from severe perceptual disorders, look for your own way of getting here, and when you find it, could you please bring some cards, cause we're getting pretty tired of the marbles.

chapter one

in which Mordy finds a job and a hard-core bar

Two days after I killed myself I found a job here at some pizza joint. It's called Kamikaze, and it's part of a chain. My shift manager was cool by me and helped me find a place to live, with this German guy who works at the same store. The job's no big deal, but it'll do for a while. And this place—I don't know—whenever they used to sound off about life after death and go through the whole is-there-isn't-there routine, I never thought about it one way or the other. But I'll tell you this much: even when I thought there was, I'd always imagine these beeping sounds, like a fuzz-buster, and people floating around in space and stuff. But now that I'm here, I don't know, mostly it reminds me of Tel Aviv. My room-mate, the German, says this place could just as well be Frankfurt. I guess Frankfurt's a dump, too. By the time it got dark, I'd found a bar—an OK place called Stiff Drinks. The music wasn't bad, either—not exactly up to date, but with character and lots of girls chilling on their own. On some of them you could tell straight off how they did it, with the scars on their wrists and everything, but there were some that looked really good. One of them—definitely hot—

came on to me right on the first night. Her skin was kinda loose like, kinda droopy. Like someone who'd done it drowning, but she had a bod to die for, and her eyes were something else. I didn't make a move, though. Kept telling myself it was because of Desiree. 'Cause dying and all just made me love her more. But who knows, maybe I'm just repressed.

chapter two
in which Mordy meets a real friend and loses a
game of pool

I met Uzi Gelfand at Stiff Drinks, almost by accident. He acted real friendly. Bought me a beer and everything, which weirded me out 'cause I figured he must be trying to stick it to me or something. But pretty soon I saw he wasn't on to me at all, just bored. He was a few years older than me and going bald, so the little scar—the one on his right temple where the bullet went in—stuck out even more, and so did the other one, which was much bigger, on the left side, where it went out. "Used a dumdum," Gelfand goes and winks at two girls standing at the bar right next to us, drinking Diet Coke. "I mean if you're gonna do it, do it right." It wasn't until after those two ditched us for some blond guy with a ponytail that he admitted he'd only chatted me up 'cause he thought we were together. "Not that it makes any difference," he says, and head-butts the bar—but not very hard, just trying to chill, "even if you'd introduced me they'da gone off with some blond guy in the end. That's just how it is. Every girl I meet—they always have a blond guy waiting for them somewhere. But I'm not bitter. No way. A little desperate, maybe, but not bitter." Four beers later we were shooting pool, and Uzi started telling me about himself. Turned out he was living not far away from my place, but with his parents, which was pretty weird. I mean most people live alone here, or with a girlfriend maybe, or a roommate. Uzi's parents had committed suicide five years before him. His mother had some disease and his father didn't want to go on without her. His little brother was also living with them. Just got here. Shot himself too, in the middle of basic training. "Maybe I shouldn't say this," Uzi smiled and potted the eight ball right into the left pocket, on a fluke, "but when he got here we were really stoked. You shoulda seen my dad, a guy who wouldn't bat an eye if you dropped a ten-pound sledgehammer on his foot. Grabbed the kid and cried like a baby, no shit."

chapter three

in which Kurt starts bitching and Mordy's had
enough

Ever since I met Uzi we hit the bars every
night. There's only like three of them here and we
hit all three each time just to be sure we don't miss
out on any action. We always wind up at Stiff Drinks.
It's the best one, and it stays open latest, too. Last
night really sucked. Uzi brought this friend of his,
Kurt. Thinks the guy's really cool cause he was the
leader of some famous band and everything. But the
truth is he's a big-time jerk. I mean, I'm not exactly
sold on the place either, but this guy, he wouldn't
stop bitching. And once he gets going—forget it.
He'll dig into you like a goddam bat. Anything that
comes up always reminds him of some song he wrote,
and he's gotta recite it for you so you can tell him
how cool the lyrics are. Sometimes he'll even ask the
bartender to play one of his numbers and you just
wanna dig yourself a hole in the ground. It isn't just
me. Everybody hates him, except Uzi. I think there's
this thing that after you off yourself, with the way it
hurts and everything—and it hurts like hell—the last
thing you give a shit about is somebody with nothing
on his mind except singing about how unhappy he

is. I mean if you gave a flyin' fuck about stuff like that you'd still be alive, with a depressing poster of Nick Cave over your bed, instead of winding up here. But the truth is that it isn't only him. Yesterday I was just bummed out. The job at the pizza joint and pissing the night away at the bars, it was all getting pretty tired. Seeing the same people with their flat Coke every night, and even when they'd look you straight in the eye you'd feel like they were just kinda staring. I don't know, maybe I'm too uptight, but when you look at them, even when you feel the vibes in the air like something's really happening, and they're dancing, or making out or having some laughs with you, somehow there's always this thing about them, like it's never a big deal, like nothing really matters.

chapter four

Dinner at the Gelfands

On Friday Uzi invited me over to his parents' place for dinner. "Eight o'clock sharp," he said, "and don't be late. We're having bean and potato *cholent* with *kishke*." You could tell the Gelfands were from Eastern Europe. The furniture was a DIY job that Uzi's father put together, and they had these god-awful stucco walls. I didn't really wanna go. Parents always think I'm a bad influence. I don't know why. Take the first time I had dinner at Desiree's house. Her father kept looking me over, like I was some punk trying to get a driver's license and he was the guy from the DMV who wasn't going to let me pass. By the time we got to dessert, he was ragging on me—but trying to make like it was no big deal—to see if I was into getting his daughter to do drugs. "I know how it goes," he said, giving me that undercover cop look—the kind they give just before they cuff you. "I used to be young too, you know. You go to a party, dance a little, things get heated up, and next thing you know you're in some room together, and you're getting her to take a kote." "A toke," I tried to tell him. "Whatever. Listen, Mordy, I may seem naive, but I know the routine." I lucked out with the Gelfands, though, 'cause those kids were so far gone that their parents had nothing left to worry about. They were really happy to have me there and kept trying to stuff me with food. There's something nice about home cooking. I mean it's hard to explain, but there's something special about it, a feeling. As if your stomach can figure out that it's food you didn't have to pay for, that someone actually made it out of love. And after all those pizza joints and Chinese takeouts and junk that my stomach's taken in since I got here, it appreciated the gesture. To thank me, it sent these heat waves up to my chest every once in a while. "She's a real shark, our mom,"

Uzi went, and he hugged his tiny mother real tight without even letting go of the silverware. Uzi's mom laughed and asked if we wanted some more *kishke*, his father got in another lame joke, and for a second there I actually started missing my own parents, even though before I offed myself their nagging used to freak me out.

chapter five

in which Mordy and Gelfand's kid brother do the dishes

After dinner I sat in the living room with the rest of them. Uzi's dad turned on the TV. There was this boring talk show on, and he kept swearing at everyone on the show. Uzi'd had a whole bottle of wine with his dinner and just passed out on the couch. It was getting pretty tired, so me and Uzi's kid brother Ronny said we'd do the dishes even though Uzi's mom said don't bother. Ronny washed and I dried. I asked him how he's makin' out 'cause I know he offed not so long ago, and people are usually pretty much in a daze when they get here, at least in the beginning. But Ronny just shrugged and said he thinks OK. Then he said: "If it hadn't been for Uzi, I'da been here a long time ago." We did all the dishes and we were putting them away when Ronny started telling me this really weird story about how once, when he was just ten maybe, he took a cab, on his own, to see the two Tel Aviv soccer teams play each other. He was dead gone on the yellow team, with the hats and the pennants and everything, and all through the game they were right on top of the other side's goal. Those guys couldn't keep the ball for two passes in a row. But then, eight minutes before the end of the game, the other team scored an offside goal. No two ways about it. It was such an obvious offside—like the replays they show on TV. The yellows tried to argue, but the referee gave the goal and that was that. The other team won, and Ronny went home totally burned up. Uzi was hung up on fitness in those days. He was going into the army, and he was dead set on trying out for a combat unit. And Ronny, who idolized him, took his jump rope, tied it to the horizontal bar that Uzi put up in the yard, and made a noose. Then he shouted to Uzi, who was cramming for some final or something, to come right away and told him the whole thing about the game, and about the goal and about how unfair it was and everything, and how he didn't see the point of going on living in a world that's so unfair that the team you love could lose just like that, even when they didn't deserve to. And that he was only telling Uzi because Uzi was probably the smartest guy Ronny knew, so unless Uzi could give him one good reason to go on living, he was gonna off himself and that was that. The whole time Ronny talked Uzi didn't say a word, and even afterward, when it was his turn to say something, he just kept quiet, and instead of talking, he took one step forward and slapped Ronny so hard that it sent him flying two yards back, and then he just turned around and went back to his room to cram some more. Ronny says it took him a while to get over being slapped, but soon as he got up he untied the rope and put it back and went to take a shower. He never talked to Uzi about the meaning of life again after that. "I don't know exactly what he was trying to tell me when he slapped me like that," Ronny said, laughing, and wiped his hands on the dish towel, "but whatever it was, it worked fine till the army."

chapter six
in which Mordy stops barhopping and starts losing it

I haven't done the bars for almost two weeks. Uzi keeps calling anyway, bugging me about how I'm missing out on the babes and the laughs, and he promises not to bring Kurt along, but so far I'm sitting tight. Once every three days, he even comes to see me at like three A.M., helps himself to a beer and tells me some funny story I should've heard at the bar or about some waitress he almost hooked up with. He never leaves anything out, like when some kid misses school and another kid comes over to tell him what they have to do for homework. And then, just before he leaves he tries to talk me into going out for a little espresso before we crash. Last night I told him I'd had it with those places, that we never get anywhere with the chicks anyway, and that I just get bummed out. "As if you're not bummed out anyway," Uzi goes. "Look at yourself, vegging in front of the TV every morning like a baboon. Get this, Mordy. The fact that nothing happens is a given. But as long as nothing happens, at least let it be in a place with babes and some music. Right?"

After he left, I tried reading this really depressing book my German roommate lent me—about a guy with TB who went to this place in Italy to spend his dying days. After twenty-three pages I junked it and turned on the TV. They had a game show on, where the contestants meet people who offed on the same date and they all have to say why—but it has to be funny—and what they'd do with the first prize if they won. I figured maybe Uzi was right—just vegging out at home isn't so hot either, and that unless something happened, and soon, I was going to freak out.

chapter seven

in which Mordy accidentally foils a robbery and
almost wins a reward

The day everything began changing started with me foiling a robbery. I know it sounds like
I'm making it up almost, but it really happened. I'd
just finished buying some stuff at the supermarket
when this fat guy with red hair and a thick scar on
his neck slammed right into me, and about twenty
TV dinners fell out of his coat. Both of us just froze.
I think I was more shook up than him. The cashier
next to us yelled: "Simon! Come over here, quick.
Thief! Thief!" I wanted to tell the fat guy I was sorry
and that I was happy for him he wasn't really fat. That
I only thought he was on account of the TV dinners
in his coat, and that next time he shoplifts he should
stick to vegetables cause meat always comes out wet
and disgusting in the microwave. But I just shrugged,
and the fat guy, who was looking pretty skinny by
then, shrugged too, the way only someone with a broken neck can, and then he bailed out. Right after
that Simon came running over, waving a stick, and
gave this really sad look at the TV dinners that were
scattered all over the floor. "How could he?" he whispered, getting down on his hands and knees, half to

me and half to the frozen peas that were rolling all over the place. "How can anyone do a thing like that? Shoplifting's one thing, but stepping on moussaka?! What good is that?" Before I could get outta there, the cashier was all over me. "Boy, was that lucky! Good thing you were here! Look at him, Simon, this is the guy who caught the thief." And Simon's like: "Terrific," but he goes on staring at the crushed moussaka. "Terrific. Superdeal Stores thanks you. If you would be so kind as to step into my office and leave me your name and . . ." "They'll make it worth your while," the cashier pitched in. "There's a reward." Simon was busy trying to pick up the TV dinners and work out the damage. I smiled at the cashier and told her thanks a lot, but never mind, and besides I gotta be somewhere and I can't wait. "You sure?" she asked, disappointed. I could tell she was really cut up about it. "It's a pretty neat reward. A weekend at a hotel." When I told Gelfand, he nearly shit a brick. "A weekend at a hotel?" He peeled himself a banana. "Couldn't be more obvious than that. The girl's got it for you." "Chill out," I said. "It's just store policy." "What did she look like?" Gelfand ignored me. "Was she hot?" "She was OK, I guess, but . . ." "No buts," he insisted. "Spit it out. How old did she look?" "Twenty-five," I gave in. "Visible scars? Slash marks? Bullet holes, that kinda thing?" "Not that I could see." "A Juliet!" Gelfand whistled in admiration. Juliet's the word they use here for anyone who did it with pills or poison, like me, the ones who get here with no scars. "Young *and* a Juliet *and* hot too. . . ." "I didn't say she was hot," I protested. "C'mon," Gelfand wouldn't let it go. He put on his disgusting leather piece. "Where to?" I asked, trying to stall. "Superdeal," he announced. "Let's go get the reward they owe us." "Us?" I asked. "Just come on and stop jawing," Gelfand commanded, doing his Mr. Big thing. So I shut up and went.

At Superdeal they had a new shift. Simon and the cashier weren't there anymore, and the others didn't know what we were talking about. Gelfand tried arguing for a while, but it was becoming a real drag and I went to get us some beers. Next to the carp tank I met Hayim, who was my roomie when I was still alive. I certainly wasn't expecting to see him here. I mean like Hayim was just about the sorriest excuse for a human being that I'd ever met, the kind of roommate that could get all pissed off over a couple of hairs in the sink or if you ate some of his cottage cheese. But he was also the last person in the world you'd ever expect to kill himself. I made like I didn't see him and just kept on going, but he spotted me and shouted, so I had to stop. "Mordy! I was hoping we'd meet up sooner or later." "Hey, man," I forced a smile. "Hayim, wassup? What're you doing here?" "Same as everyone else," Hayim mumbled.

"Same as everyone else. It's even got something to do with you." "What happened?" I asked. "Did I forget to clean up the kitchen before I offed, or something?" "You always were a million laughs, Mordy," Hayim said, and then he went into every detail of how he jumped out the window, straight from our apartment on the fourth floor to the sidewalk below. And how the whole time he kept hoping it would be over right away, but he fell lopsided—half on a neighbor's car and half on this hedge—and it took like hours till it was over. I told him I still didn't get what it had to do with me, and he said it didn't exactly have anything to do with me, but in a way it did. "Y'know," he said and arched his back till his head reached the cereal shelf. "You know how they say suicides always happen in threes. Well, there's something to it. People around you start dying, and you begin to ask yourself what the hell makes you different, and what's keeping you alive, anyway. It hit me like a Scud. I mean I just didn't have the answers. It wasn't you so much, it was more Desiree." "Desiree?" I cut in. "Yeah, Desiree. About a month after you. I was sure you knew." Behind the counter, one of the Superdeal workers was whacking this carp on the head with a mallet, and I could feel the tears streaming down my face. I hadn't cried even once since I got here. "Don't take it so hard," Hayim said and touched me with his sweaty hand. "The doctors said she didn't feel a thing. Know what I mean, it was over right away." "Who's taking it hard, man?" I kissed him on the forehead. "She's here, get it? All I gotta do is find her." I could see the shift manager in the back, explaining something to Gelfand, who was nodding and looking kind of bored. I guess even he finally figured out we weren't getting any reward.

chapter eight
in which Uzi tries to teach Mordy something about life and gives up

You don't have a living chance of finding her," Gelfand said and helped himself to a beer. "I'll bet you anything." "A beer," I smiled and went on packing my bag. "A beer," Gelfand mimicked. "D'you have any idea how many bods they got out there, you airhead? You're clueless. Me and you have been going back and forth for God knows how long on this two-by-two piece of shit, and we still don't know half the people here. So just where are you gonna look for her? In Kingdom Come? This Genevieve of yours might be living right next door." "Desiree," I corrected. "Desiree, Genevieve, Marie-Claire. What's the difference?" Gelfand opened his beer on a corner of the table. "Just another rich piece of ass." "Suit yourself," I answered and went on packing. Last thing I

genius?" "I'm not trying to diss you, Mordy. I'm just trying to tell you something. I dunno, like I'm not even sure what it is." Gelfand sat down beside me. "Lemme put it this way. Since you got here, how many times d'you get laid?" "Why?" "Just because." "Actually laid? None, I think." "You think?" "None," I confessed. "But what's that got to do with it?" "Plenty. Because you're up to your eyeballs with sperm, got that? Everything you look at is gray. Your sperm count's so high and your brain's pressing against your skull so hard that you think you're having an out-of-body experience like nobody in the whole goddam universe ever had before. Like you're so strung out it's worth dying for. Leaving everything. Going off to live in the Galilee. Ever live in the Galilee? You know, nothing but goat shit and once-a-day buses." "Lay off, Uzi. I really don't need this, you know," I cut in. "Just gimme the car, OK? And don't start bitching about the insurance. If I break anything, I'll pay for it." "Don't go getting touchy on me all of a sudden," Gelfand shot back and patted me on the shoulder. "All I said was that it's not a good enough reason. I didn't say I wouldn't come with you. Maybe you're right. Maybe I'm just bullshitting you. Maybe this Irma really is something special. . . ." "Desiree," I corrected him again. "Right," Gelfand smiled. "Sorry." "Know what? Forget about rich bitches and love and all that shit," I tried a different tack. "I've got another reason for you to come." "Try me," Gelfand shot the empty beer bottle in the garbage can and tried to sound interested. "You got anything better to do?"

chapter nine

in which the two friends go looking for Desiree and find Arabs instead

Gelfand promised his parents he'd call every day, and right from the first block he started looking for a phone. "Take it easy, man," I told him. "You been in South America, you been in India, you blew your brains out with a dumdum slug. Stop behaving like a fucking Boy Scout at summer camp." "Get off my case, Mordy. I'm warning you," Gelfand snarled and kept driving. "Just look at this place. Get a load of the characters around here. Tell you the truth, I dunno why I came with you." The people outside looked a lot like the ones in our neighborhood—their eyes kinda dim, and dragging their feet. The only difference was that Gelfand didn't know them—which was enough to make him paranoid. "I'm not being paranoid. Don't you get it? They're all Arabs." "So what if they're Arabs?" I asked. "So what? I dunno. Arabs—suicides—doesn't that psych you out, even a little? What if they figure out we're

Israeli?" "I guess they'll kill us again. Can't you get it into your skull they don't give a flyin' fuck? They're dead. We're dead. *Finito la comedia.*" "I dunno," Gelfand muttered. "I don't like Arabs. It isn't even politics. It's something ethnic." "Tell me something, Uzi. Aren't you fucked up enough without being a racist, too?" "I'm not a racist," Gelfand squirmed. "I just . . . know what? Maybe I am a little racist. But just a little." It was getting dark, and the lights in Gelfand's beat-up old Chevy had been dead for a long time, so we had to stop for the night. He locked the doors from the inside and made us rack out in the car. We moved the seats back and tried to make like we were just about to zonk out. Once in a while Uzi even went through the whole toss-and-turn routine. It was really pathetic. After an hour, even he had had enough. He pulled the seat back up and said: "C'mon, let's go find a bar." "What about the Arabs?" "Screw the Arabs," he said. "If worse comes to worse, we'll let 'em have it. Like in the army." "You were never in the army," I reminded him. "You were section eight, which kinda figures." "Same difference," Uzi got out of the Chevy and slammed the door. "I saw how they do it on TV."

curity Forces thing? Were you in the army?" he asked as he poured. "Sure," Uzi lied. "Undercover unit . . . three straight years of battle rations, day in and day out!" Nasser handed Uzi the beer, and when he brought me mine he whispered: "He's not all there, your friend, is he?" "I guess you could say that," I smiled. "Never mind," Nasser reassured me. "That's why he's so—what's the word? Irresistible." "The guy's unreal!" Uzi said and downed half a glass in one go. "Me—irresistible!" "He was never really in the army, and it's eating him up," I explained. "Sure I was," Uzi argued. "I even reenlisted. The gun—" he said, pointing to the hole in his temple and making like he was shooting a pistol, "my service weapon. Say, Nasser, how'd you close up shop?" Uzi was obviously trying to pick a fight, 'cause if there's one thing you're never supposed to ask around here it's how they offed. But this Nasser guy looked so wasted that even Uzi couldn't rattle him. "Kaboom!" he smiled faintly and wiggled his mangled body a little. "Can't you tell?" "No shit," Uzi said. "Kaboom! How many'd you take with you?" Nasser shook his head and poured himself a vodka. "How should I know?" "You're pulling my leg," Uzi was all shook up. "You never even asked? Somebody musta gotten here after you." "It's not the kind of thing you ask," Nasser said and downed the shot of vodka. "Tell me where and when it was," Uzi nagged. "If I was after you, maybe

I could tell you how many . . ." "Drop it," Nasser stiffened for a moment. "What for?" "Hey," I made a move to change the subject, "it's packed here tonight." "Yeah, dynamite," Nasser smiled. "It's like this every night. Trouble is it's almost all guys. Every once in a while you get a couple of chicks. A tourist maybe. But hardly any." "Say," Uzi pressed on, "is it true that when you people go out on a job they promise you seventy nymphomaniac virgins in Kingdom Come? All for you, *solico*?" "Sure, they promise," Nasser said, "and look what it got me. Lukewarm vodka." "So you're just a sucker in the end, eh, *ya* Nasser," Uzi gloated. "Sure thing," Nasser nodded. "And you, what did they promise you?"

chapter eleven
in which Mordy dreams about him and Desiree
buying a couch, and has a rude awakening

That night, in the car, I dreamt that Desiree and me are buying a couch, and the salesman is the Arab from the bar, the one Uzi kept hassling. He shows us all kinds of couches, and we can't decide on one we both like. The one Desiree wants is really gross, with red upholstery and everything, and I want something else—I can't remember what, exactly. And we get into an argument right there in the store.

We're not just discussing it. We're yelling. And it gets uglier and uglier, and we start saying things that really hurt, and then, in the dream, suddenly I get hold of myself and I stop short. "Let's not fight," I say. "It doesn't matter. Just a stupid couch, that's all. The only thing that matters is that we're together." And when I say it, she smiles, and then, instead of smiling back, I wake up in the car. Uzi's on the seat next to me, and he's tossing and turning in his sleep, cursing all sorts of people who were bugging him in his dream. "Stuff it," he was telling someone who must have really gone too far. "One more word and you'll have a mud pie on your head." I guess the guy just kept going, cause Uzi tried to get up and caught the steering wheel in the ribs. With him awake too, we opened the windows and had a smoke. "Tomorrow we're getting a wigwam or an igloo, or whatever you call that piece of plastic shit they sell at camping supplies stores," Uzi announced. "A tent," I said. "Yeah, a tent. That's the last time we sleep in the car." Uzi took one more puff and threw the butt out the window. "He was an OK guy, actually, that Arab in the bar. The beer was shit but that Nasser was pretty sharp. You know what I was dreaming about?" "Yeah," I said and took a drag of what was left of the cigarette, "that you're crapping on his head."

her backpack on the backseat and climbing in. I shrugged. "You got a clue where you're going?" "You haven't been here long, I guess," Uzi laughed. "Why's that?" she asked, kinda pissed. " 'Cause otherwise you'd've figured out by now that nobody here has a clue. Maybe if we did, we wouldn't be here in the first place." Her name was Leehee, and she told us that she really did just get here and that she's been thumbing rides the whole time, because she's gotta find the people in charge. "The people in charge?!" Uzi laughed. "What do you think this is, a goddam country club, where you go to the main office? This place is just like before you offed, only a little bit worse. By the way, when you were still alive, d'you ever go looking for God?" "No," Leehee said and offered me some gum. "But I didn't really have any reason to." "And what reason do you have now?" Uzi laughed and took some gum too. "You're sorry you did it? 'Cause you know, if that's it, and you're all ready with your backpack and everything and you're just waiting for someone to hand you the visa back home . . ." "Tell me," I butted in before he started getting really mean. "Why'd you wait till we passed you before you stuck out your thumb?" "I don't know," Leehee shrugged. "I guess I wasn't sure I wanted to hitch a ride with you. When I saw you from far away I thought you looked a little . . ." "Mean?" Uzi suggested. "No," Leehee smiled awkwardly. "Obnoxious."

since she joined us everything had been getting really heavy. "Neither one of us is gonna score with her anyway, y'know," he said and wrung it out. "But at least when we were on our own we could dish the dirt." "Dish the dirt all you want," I said. "Who's stopping you?" "Basically you're right," Uzi admitted, "but deep down we both know that shoveling the shit just isn't the same when there's a babe around. Somehow it always sounds less like you mean it and more like you're all jive." When we got back to the car, I took over the wheel. All this time, Leehee was asleep in her sweats in the backseat. From the time we picked her up, I'd never seen her wearing anything with short sleeves. Uzi said he'd bet the Chevy she slashed her wrists, but neither of us had the guts to ask her how she offed and everything, and why. Not that it matters much. She's cute when she's sleeping, kind of peaceful like, and except for the bit about finding the people in charge, which is way bizotic if you ask me, she's cool. Uzi can go on bitching all he wants, but personally I think he's got a thing for her. Maybe that's really why he doesn't let it go, so I don't catch on. Truth is, sometimes I think about it myself, that maybe I won't ever find Desiree, and that maybe Leehee will fall in love with me a little too, but I snap out of it right away. Besides, I have this hunch that Desiree's real close. Uzi says that's a bunch of crap, that she's probably way on the other side, and that

don't know what you're more of—naive or brilliant. D'you have any idea how many mechanics got under the hood of this old ride? Forget mechanics. Nuclear engineers, holistic healers of heavy machinery, people who can take apart a Mack diesel engine and put it back together again in twenty seconds blindfolded couldn't fix it, till you got here." He was massaging her neck. "My angel genius." From where I sat it looked like Uzi'd chilled a little by then and he was just using the chance to go on pawing her. "You know what this means?" I said. "It means we can keep on driving at night now, too." "No shit!" Uzi said. "And the first place we go tonight with these painfully beautiful headlights is to get trashed." We kept on going, looking for a bar. Once you got out of town, things were pretty dead. Every half hour or so we'd pass a sign for some hamburger joint or pizza place.

After four hours Uzi'd had it, and we stopped to celebrate at this place that sold ice cream and frozen yogurt. Uzi asked what they had that was the closest to alcohol, and the salesgirl said it was cherry liqueur ice cream. "Hey, Sandra," Uzi said after he took a peek at her name tag, "how many cones d'you think we'd have to have to really get trashed?" Under her name on the tag was their logo—a seal in a clown's hat riding a unicycle, and under that was the motto: "Low in price, high in flavor." "I dunno," Sandra shrugged. "Then give us ten pints," Uzi said. "Just to be sure." Sandra was real good at filling the containers. She looked kind of worn out, but her eyes were wide open the whole time, almost like she was constantly surprised. Whatever she did to off herself, it must have been sudden. On our way to the car, Leehee stopped next to this poster listing all the things the workers were supposed to remember: Be polite to customers. Wash your hands after using the bathroom. That kind of thing. We had one like that at the Kamikaze, right next to the can, and I never washed my hands when I took a shit. No reason—just to feel like I was doing my own thing. "Places like that really get me down," Leehee said back in the car, after we'd had some of the ice cream. "I go in hoping something unexpected will happen. Something small even. Like a salesperson wearing a name tag upside down or forgetting to put on a hat, or just going, 'Give yourself a break—the food here really sucks.' But it never actually happens. Know what I mean?" "Frankly," Uzi grabbed the ice cream away from her, "not really. Want me to drive?" You could tell he was dying to take the wheel, with the new lights and everything. Less than a mile after he took over, there was a sharp turn to the right and just beyond it was this tall, thin guy with glasses sprawled right in the middle of the road, fast asleep. He went right on snoring—even after Uzi swerved right off the road and wrapped the car around a tree. We got out. Nobody was hurt, but the Chevy was a total wreck. "Hey, you," Uzi screamed, running toward the guy and shaking him. "You crazy or something?" "Vice versa," he said. In like a second, the guy was wide awake and up on his feet. He held out his hand to Uzi. "I'm Raphael. Raphael Kneller. But you guys can call me Rafi." When he saw that Uzi wasn't taking his hand, he squinted and asked: "What's that smell? Like ice cream." And right after that, without waiting for an answer: "You haven't seen a dog around here by any chance; have you?"

chapter fifteen

in which Kneller extends lots of hospitality and a little paranoia, and explains why his house isn't really a camp

After Uzi'd calmed down a little, we checked out the car and saw it was totaled. Kneller was all shook up 'cause of what happened and 'cause it was all his fault. He said he wanted us to come crash at his place anyway. He didn't stop blabbing the whole way, and every step he took, his body went in all directions like he was trying to go lots of different places at the same time and couldn't make up his mind. One thing's for sure, he looked completely crazy, this Kneller, but harmless. He even smelled kinda fresh and innocent, like a baby's bottom. I couldn't picture a guy like that offing himself. "I'm not usually out at this hour, but I was looking for my dog Freddie. He's lost. D'you see him by any chance? It's just that suddenly all the peace and quiet around here started really getting to me. Well, whadda you expect? Everyone likes to veg out in the woods, know what I mean, in the great outdoors and everything," Kneller tried to explain, waving his arms around a lot. "But why that way? Why in the middle of the fucking road, dammit? I mean it's fucking irresponsible, if you ask me." "Too many recreational drugs, I guess," he winked at us, and when he saw that Uzi was still really pissed off and looking pretty peeved, he added quickly: "Metaphorically, I mean. Nobody really does drugs around here." Kneller's house looked just like those stupid little houses we used to draw in kindergarten, with a red roof and a chimney, a green tree in the yard and a yellowish light in the windows. There was an enormous sign over the doorway, with FOR RENT on it in big bold letters, and KNELLER'S HAPPY CAMPERS scribbled in blue paint right over that. Kneller told us that the house wasn't really for rent, or actually, that it used to be for rent once but that then Kneller came along and rented it, and it isn't like he even runs a camp. It's just a joke, not a very funny one, that a friend of his made up. This friend used to live with him for a long time, and he figured because of all the company that kept coming and all the fun stuff that Kneller used to set up for them, that this place was kinda like a camp. "Wait till they see the ice cream," he smiled, and he pointed to the container that Leehee was holding. "They'll freak out."

chapter sixteen
in which Leehee performs a small miracle and Uzi falls in love with an Eskimo

It's been almost a month since we got here. Kneller's starting to get used to the idea that his dog Freddie isn't planning to come back, and it doesn't look like the tow truck that Gelfand ordered is ever going to show up either. During the first week, Uzi was still driving everybody crazy and dialing all sorts of numbers to figure out a way of getting back home, but then he met this Eskimo. She was way cute and was from too far away to pick up on his character. Ever since they've been an item he's less hung up on getting out of here, and even though he still calls his mom and dad every day, now mostly he talks about her. At first this place really got to me, too, with its cheerleader types from all over, who only after they offed discovered that this place was actually the flip side of a blast. Kind of like a cross between United

hoeing the flowerbeds. "Miracles?" I asked. "Because you know, Rafi, it isn't like Leehee turned water into wine, but it comes pretty close." "Not close enough," Kneller said. "You wanna give it a name? Call it a miracle, but it's not a significant one. Miracles like that are no biggie around here. Strange you even noticed. Most people don't." Leehee and I didn't really get it. But Kneller explained that one of the things about this place was that people can do pretty amazing stuff like turning stones into plants, or changing animals' colors, or even floating in the air a little. But only so long as it's not significant and it doesn't count for anything. I told him that was pretty amazing and that if it was really happening so much around here, then we could try putting together some kind of a show, like a magic act or something, maybe even getting it on television. "But that's what I'm trying to tell you," Kneller said and kept scuffing the ground. "You can't do that, 'cause as soon as people come specially to see it, it won't work. These things only work if they don't really matter. It's like, say, you find yourself suddenly walking on water, which is something that happens here every now and then, but only if there's nothing waiting for you on the other side, or if there's no one around who's gonna get all worked up about it." Leehee told him about what happened to the headlights the night we met, and Kneller said it was a perfect example. "Fix-

wham!—there you are with scars and a mortgage.
And why only suicides, anyway? Why not regular dead
people too? Like somehow the whole thing doesn't
make any sense. Take it or shove it, know what I
mean? And even if it's not that groovy, things coulda
been a lot worse. Uzi's spending all his time with his
new girlfriend. There's this river not far from here,
and she's teaching him how to kayak and fish, which
is pretty weird, 'cause I for one never heard or saw
any animals around here practically, except for
Kneller's dog maybe. And for all I know that dog may
not even exist, either. Uzi doesn't have much to offer
her in return, but just so he doesn't feel like a
shmuck he's teaching her the names of all the late
greats of soccer, and how to swear in Arabic. And
me—most of the time I'm with Leehee. Kneller's got
these bikes in his storeroom, and we go biking a lot.
She told me about how she offed. Turns out she
didn't kill herself at all. She just ODed. Somebody
talked her into shooting up. It was the first time for
both of them, and they probably botched it. That's
why she's convinced it's all a mistake and that if she
could just find one of the people in charge and explain, they'd transfer her out of here right away.
Truth is, I don't think she has a chance of finding
anyone like that, but I think I'd better not tell her.
Leehee asked me not to talk about it to anyone but
I told Uzi, and Uzi said it was a crock of shit and that

of the cell was pretty easy, but once we got to the
yard, there were all these sirens and floodlights and
stuff. The van was waiting for us on the other side,
and I helped lift Uzi and Leehee to climb over. But
when I wanted to climb over myself, there was nobody left to help me, and then suddenly I see Kneller,
and before I can even ask him, he just floats up in
the air and over to the other side. Everybody's out
by then, including Desiree, who's driving the van,
and they're all just waiting for me. I can hear the
sirens and the dogs behind me, and all the other
stuff you always hear in prison films, and they're clos-
ing in on me. And Uzi keeps screaming at me from
the other side: "Shit, Mordy, what is it with you? Just
float a little." And just to like piss me off, Kneller
keeps floating back and forth over the van, doing all
kinds of loops and back-flips and stuff, and I try too
but I just can't cut it. Then they all drive off, or else
Uzi's family shows up. Truth is, I don't really remember what happens after that. "You know what that
dream's trying to tell you?" Uzi says. "That you're
screwed up. A pushover, and screwed up too. A pushover, because all I have to do is say the word 'slam-
mer' once, and you go and have a dream about it.
And screwed up, cause that's what the dream itself
says."

Uzi and me are sitting by the river holding a
clothesline and trying to fish with some trick his girl-

friend taught him. We've been sitting there for like two hours, and nothing. Not even a fucking shoe, which is what's really ticking him off. "Just think about it. In your dream, everyone gets out 'cause they don't take their existence seriously. But you, you're so busy obsessing that you're just stuck. That dream's open and shut. Almost educational, if you ask me." It's getting cold, and I'm beginning to wonder when Uzi will ever get tired of this fishing shit, 'cause to tell the truth, I got fed up a long time ago, and it's pretty obvious there are no fish here. "Let me tell you something else," Uzi went on. "It's not just your dream. It's that you remember it and rag about it. There's lots of people with dreams but they don't get all tight-assed. I have dreams too, y'know, but I don't go making you listen to them, and that's why I'm a happier person." And then, like he has to prove his point, he gives his line a pull, and there's this fish at the end of it. Small and ugly but big enough to inflate Uzi's overinflated ego even more. "Listen to a friend for a chance. Forget your dumb dreams and those retarded miracles. Now's the knowing. Go for Leehee. Why not? She looks good. A little spacey maybe but nice, and she's hot for you, that's for sure. Take it from me, she's never going to find God and file her complaint, and you're never going to find your rich piece of dead ass. You're both stuck here on your own, so you might as well make the most of it." The ugly fish was squirming on Uzi's line. Suddenly it changed into something else, red and a little bigger but just as ugly. Uzi held it down and bashed its head with a stone to make it stop flopping, which is another Eskimo trick. He didn't even notice how it changed. To tell the truth, maybe he's right. Maybe it really doesn't fucking matter. But when it comes to Desiree, I just know she's here. It's like all I have to do is turn around and she'll be there behind me. And I don't give a shit how much Uzi rides me, 'cause I just know I'm going to find her. "Tell me one thing," Uzi says on our way home. "This Kneller, what gives with him? Why is he always so fucking stoked, and hugging people and stuff? Is he gay or what?"

chapter nineteen

in which Kneller has a birthday party and Mordy and Leehee decide to move on

More and more people keep arriving, cause Kneller's supposed to be having this birthday blast and everyone's all psyched up—baking cakes or dreaming up far-out things to give him. Most of them are so uncoordinated you wonder how they even breathe, and Leehee says we'll be damn lucky if all this creative hullabaloo doesn't get anyone hurt. So far, two of them cut themselves and another guy is bleeding from every finger cause he was trying to sew Kneller a bag. And then there's this Dutch space cadet, Jan. Yesterday he grabbed a butterfly net and said he was going to catch Kneller a new dog in the woods. Hasn't been heard from since. Kneller's happy as a pig in shit. In the evening, we were like setting the table for this blowout meal, and I asked him how old he was, and he started to kind of stutter, 'cause suddenly he discovered he couldn't remember. After all the grub and the presents, they played some CDs and people actually danced, like it was a fucking prom or something. I even slow-danced with Leehee. At about four in the morning, someone remembered that Kneller used to play the fiddle and that his old violin was just lying there in the storeroom. At first he wouldn't play, but pretty soon he gave in and played "Knockin' on Heaven's Door." Truth is I don't know shit about music, but I never in my life heard anyone play like that. It's not that he didn't miss a couple of notes. He did. But you could tell by the sound that he was really sincere about what he was playing. It wasn't only me. Everyone just stood there and listened and didn't say a word, like when there's a moment of silence for someone that died. Even Uzi, the original killjoy, kept quiet, and his eyes were watery. He told me later it was his allergies, but you could see he was just saying that. After Kneller finished playing, nobody wanted to do much anymore. Mostly they just hit the sack, and Leehee and me helped clean up a little. In the kitchen she asked me if I still miss all the things from before I offed. I told her the truth, that it isn't like I'm not dying to go back, but I don't remember much of anything except Desiree, and now that she's here too, there's nothing I miss. "Maybe I miss myself a little," I said. "The way I used to be before I offed. I'm probably just making this up, but I remember myself more like . . . I don't know. I can't even remember that anymore." Leehee said she missed everything, even the things she hated, and that she had to figure out how to take off by the following day, because the only way she was ever going to find someone who could help her was to keep looking. I told her she was right and that I should pack up, too, if I really wanted to find Desiree. We finished stacking the dishes in the sink, but neither of us really wanted to call it a night yet. Kneller was sitting on the living-room floor, playing with his presents like some kid. Suddenly Jan came in, all worked up, holding his dumb butterfly net, and said that the Messiah King was living on the other side of the forest and that he was holding Kneller's dog hostage.

chapter twenty

in which Freddie packs away some gyros and uses an alias

Jan stared at us, out of breath, and red and everything. We sat him down in the living room and brought him a glass of water and he told us how he got lost in the forest looking for a new dog for Kneller, and how in the end, when he came out on the other side, he saw this mansion with a swimming pool and he wanted to ask the people there to let him use the phone to call Kneller's place so that he could ask us to send someone to pick him up, but there was no phone in the mansion, just lots of music and noise, and everyone there had a ponytail and a suntan and they all looked Australian except the girls in thongs. They were real nice and gave Jan tons of food to eat and told him that the mansion belonged to the Messiah King and that all of them were in his crowd and that the Messiah King only liked techno, which was why that was the only thing they kept playing, and full blast. They said the Messiah King was also called Joshua, but everyone there called him J, 'cause one of the babes called him that once and it stuck, and that J was originally from some bumblefuck little place in the Galilee, but that he's been here forever, and there was going to be a significant miracle in a week. A planned miracle. Not something that just happened by chance. And that they couldn't say what it was but that it would be something majorly big and that Jan could stay and watch. Jan was kinda getting used to the music and was sorta into it by then, partly because of the miracle, but mainly because of all the naked babes. They fixed him up a room in the mansion with this really nice surfer who, before he offed himself, was manager of the Hard Rock Café in Wellington, New Zealand. That evening they all went skinny-dipping and Jan was kinda shy so he just stood next to the pool, but suddenly he spotted Kneller's dog, Freddie, eating gyros from a plastic dish. Jan explained that Freddie belonged to a good friend of his and that he'd been lost for a few weeks, and everyone seemed pretty confused because the Messiah King had adopted the dog and said that it was real brainy and that he even taught it to talk. Jan knew the dog could say a few words even though it didn't really understand them, anyway. But he also knew that apart from that the dog was really dumb, but he didn't want to say so because he didn't want to make the Messiah King look bad.

This Messiah King, J, was a tall, blue-eyed blond guy with long hair, and he had this girlfriend who was a little lopsided but pretty anyway, and they both listened patiently to Jan's story. Then finally J said that if the dog was lost, he'd give it back for sure,

dle of the living room and said he couldn't wait anymore. He wanted to see Freddie right away. Leehee and me offered to tag along. Leehee didn't exactly buy into the whole Messiah King thing, but she figured she had nothing to lose by asking him about the people in charge and how she could find them. And I thought if there really were as many people there as Jan said, then maybe it could be a good place to look for Desiree. Besides, Kneller and Jan were both so fucking uncoordinated that it wouldn't be a bad idea to have someone keep an eye on them. Kneller wanted us to use a bus that belonged to one of his friends, but Jan said he only knew how to get to this place on foot. Which is why we had to string along behind him through the forest for more than ten hours, till it started turning dark. That's when he had to admit he was lost. Kneller said it was a good sign, because Jan got lost last time too, and to celebrate he took out this bong, and him and Jan each took four hits, till they were totally wasted. Leehee and me decided to get some twigs to light a fire. All we had was the lighter we took from Kneller, who was sleeping like a baby. Soon as we moved away from him and Jan, who was snoring next to him, we started hearing a different sound, in the distance, like something that was breaking but was soothing too, and Leehee said it sounded to her like the sea. We headed toward it, and sure enough—a few hundred yards later we reached the beach. It was really bizarre that nobody at the camp, not even Kneller himself, ever mentioned we were near the beach. Could be they didn't know it themselves. Could be we were the only ones who knew. We took our shoes off and walked a while along the beach. Before I offed, I used to go to the beach a lot, almost every day. And when I thought about it, I got a better idea about what Leehee was saying last night—about missing things and having to go back. I told Leehee about Uzi's dad, who calls this place Deadsville, and about how the people here all seem like they don't want anything, and that most of the time when you're next to them it feels like everything is OK, when actually you're half dead already. And Leehee laughed and said that most of the people she knew, even before she offed, were either half dead or completely dead, so I was in pretty good shape. And when she said it she touched me, like it was just by accident, but it wasn't really.

I'd always hoped that if I ever cheated on Desiree, it would be with someone really pretty, so that later, when I regretted it, I could tell myself she was so beautiful that nobody would've been able to resist her. Truth is that's just how Leehee was. And that night, when she touched me, I knew she was right and that I was in pretty good shape actually.

chapter twenty-two

in which Kneller tells Freddie the whole truth to his
face

Leehee and me woke up at sunrise. Actually, we woke up cause Kneller was screaming. Soon
as we opened our eyes, we saw the beach around us
wasn't private anymore. Not that there were any people around, but now, in daylight, we discovered the
whole place was covered with used condoms. Floating
in the shallow water like jellyfish or stuck in the sand
like oysters. And suddenly everything began to smell
of used rubber. Somehow it all got swallowed up by
the smell of the sea the night before. I had to stop
myself from puking, because of Leehee. I held her
very close to me, and we just lay there like that, without moving, for I don't know how long, like a coupla
tourists stranded in a minefield, waiting to be res-
cued. "There you are," suddenly Kneller just popped
out from between the trees. "I was getting real worried. Why don't you answer when people call you?"
He led us back to where he and Jan spent the night,
and he explained on the way that this beach used to
be a hangout for hookers and druggies, except it became so grody that even hookers and druggies
couldn't take it. "Don't tell me you actually spent the

night here," he said and made a face like he couldn't believe it. Meanwhile Leehee and me wiped off the sand and everything that was sticking to our clothes. "What the hell for?" "That's how it is when you love the beach," Leehee said, giving him her half-smile. "That's how it is when you love diseases," Kneller corrected her without skipping a beat. "Just let's hope Jan doesn't get lost on us now." Sure enough, Jan was gone, but before we could start worrying about him, he came running toward us, looking totally stoked, and said he'd finally found the Messiah King's house and that it was real close.

The Messiah King's place was humongous, like all those cool houses that Desiree used to show me when we'd go visit her rich relatives in Caesarea. The kind of place where besides the swimming pool they have a squash court and a Jacuzzi, and a fallout shelter in the basement, just in case. There were more than a hundred people standing around when we got there, in a kind of a half-cocktail, half-buffet thing that must've been going on since the day before, with a lot of New Agey types, plenty of surfers, and all kinds of other characters, and everybody seemed really keyed up. Freddie kept making the rounds, pulling pitiful faces, forcing everyone to feed him, and soon as Kneller saw him he just freaked out. He stood there facing Freddie and started yelling about how could he treat him that way, and on his birthday no less, and that he was an ingrate. He started bringing up all sorts of embarrassing things that had happened when Freddie was still a pup. And all that time Freddie just looked at him calmly and went on feeding his face on this piece of sushi like some old geezer with chewing tobacco. Everyone tried to get Kneller to cool it and to tell him that J would arrive in a minute and fix everything. And when they saw it wasn't doing any good, they tried to get him interested in the miracle that J was about to perform, which only got him more hysterical. Meanwhile Leehee and me were helping ourselves to the finger food, cause we hadn't eaten all day. There was a lot we wanted to say and we pretended we weren't saying it because of the racket but we knew that wasn't the real reason. Then Jan arrived and said that J and his girlfriend wanted Kneller and Freddie to come see them in the living room to find out what this was all about, and that we'd better come too because Kneller swore he was going to raise hell. Even before we got there we could hear Kneller screaming, and there was this low doggish voice mumbling every now and then: "Cool it, man, cool it." I could pick out Desiree's voice too.

pital. Desiree told me how after my funeral she went up to the Galilee and the whole way she just cried and cried. Then, when she got to the final stop, the first thing she saw was Joshua, and as soon as she saw him something inside her became calmer, and she just stopped crying. It's not that she stopped being sad, but it wasn't hysterical anymore. It was just as deep, but something she could deal with. Joshua believed that we were all trapped in the world of the living and that there was a better world that he could get to and there were a few others who believed in his powers. Two weeks after she and Joshua met, he was supposed to separate his body from his soul, to discover the other world and to return and show everyone the way. Except that something got screwed up and his soul never made it back. At the hospital, after they'd confirmed his death, she could feel him calling her from wherever he was, which is when she took the elevator up to the roof and jumped, so that they could be together. And now they were, and Joshua was going to do it again—what he'd tried to do in the Galilee—except that this time she was sure he'd make it and that he'd find the way and he'd come back and show everyone. Then she told me again how much I meant to her, and that she knew she hurt me. She didn't know how much until after I offed, and she's glad she got to see me again so that she could ask me to forgive her. And all that time I just smiled and nodded.

kind of thing they do in movies, so I just smiled and signaled that we'd talk later. Kneller said she asked J something about how you get back to the world of the living, and J told her it was a waste of time and that he'd show everyone the way to a better world. And when they went outside, she told Kneller that this J guy was just a bullshit artist. The music was so loud, I could hardly even hear Kneller. He was laughing a little at Leehee and me. He said it was the first time he'd met people who were more naive than him. Me with my miracles, and her with her dreams. "Instead of offing," he shouted, "you should've gone to California." I saw him petting Freddie, which meant they'd made up. Joshua climbed onto the stage, wearing his long gown, and Desiree followed him, holding a kind of curvy knife, like in the Bible stories for children where Abraham is about to sacrifice Isaac. She handed the knife to Joshua and the music stopped with a bang. "What the hell is that?" Kneller muttered beside me. "The guy's dead already. What's he want now, to be double-dead?" People nearby turned around and told him to shut up. He didn't give a shit, but me, I didn't know where to put myself. Then he said he bet J would never go through with it, 'cause anyone who's offed once and knows how much it hurts to die won't try it a second time. And just when Kneller finished saying that, J took the knife and stuck it right in his heart.

chapter twenty-five

in which a white van arrives and everything comes undone

Strange, but even though everyone around the pool knew the whole time what was going to happen, it still took us all by surprise. First nobody said anything, and then people started mumbling. From where she was standing on the stage, Desiree shouted to everyone to stay calm because J would be back in his body any minute, but they went on mumbling. Meanwhile, I saw Kneller whispering to Freddie and then talking like into his lighter, and in seconds a white van pulled up and these two tall, thin guys in white overalls got out. One of them was holding a megaphone. Kneller ran toward them and started talking to them and waving his hands all over the place. I started pushing toward where the women were to look for Leehee, but I couldn't find her anywhere. The man with the megaphone asked everyone to disperse quietly. Onstage, Desiree was sitting next to J's body and crying. I saw she was trying to get to the knife, but the other guy in overalls got to it first. He took it, then he lifted J's body over his shoulder and motioned Kneller to take Desiree to the car. Again, the man with the megaphone asked the crowd to disperse. Some of them started to move, but lots of others froze. I could see Leehee now, next to the man with the megaphone. She saw me too and tried to work her way closer to me, but the driver, who was also in overalls and kept talking into some kind of radio, called her over. Leehee signaled me that she was coming in a minute, and I headed toward the van, shoving people out of the way, but by the time I got close enough, Kneller, with Freddie under his arm, and the overalls with the megaphone all got in the van and drove away. I could see Leehee in the window, trying to shout something to me, but I couldn't hear what it was. That was the last time I saw her.

chapter twenty-six
and on that optimistic note

I waited there another few hours, because at first I thought the van was only going to let J and Desiree off somewhere and that Leehee would be right back. There were still a few people hanging around. Everyone was in a daze. Nobody could really figure out what had happened. We all sat there in these deck chairs around the pool, not saying anything. Then people began to leave, one at a time, and finally when I saw I was the only one left, I headed toward Kneller's house.